THIS BOOK WILL MAKE YOU CRY

Also by Daniel Tawse

All About Romance
Emmy Star is So Everything

HODDER CHILDREN'S BOOKS

First published in Great Britain in 2025 by Hodder & Stoughton Limited

1 3 5 7 9 10 8 6 4 2

Text copyright © Daniel Tawse, 2025
Cloud image © shutterstock.com

The moral right of the author has been asserted.

*All characters and events in this publication, other than those clearly
in the public domain, are fictitious and any resemblance to
real persons, living or dead, is purely coincidental.*

All rights reserved.
No part of this publication may be reproduced, stored in
a retrieval system, or transmitted, in any form or by any means, without
the prior permission in writing of the publisher, nor be otherwise circulated
in any form of binding or cover other than that in which it is published
and without a similar condition including this condition being
imposed on the subsequent purchaser.

A CIP catalogue record for this book
is available from the British Library.

ISBN 978 1 444 97162 0

Typeset in Adobe Caslon Pro by Six Red Marbles UK, Thetford, Norfolk
Printed and bound in Great Britain by Clays Ltd, Elcograf S.p.A.

The paper and board used in this book
are made from wood from responsible sources.

Hodder Children's Books
An imprint of
Hachette Children's Group
Part of Hodder & Stoughton Limited
Carmelite House
50 Victoria Embankment
London EC4Y 0DZ

The authorised representative in the EEA is Hachette Ireland, 8 Castlecourt
Centre, Dublin 15, D15 XTP3, Ireland (email: info@hbgi.ie)

An Hachette UK Company
www.hachette.co.uk

www.hachettechildrens.co.uk

For Dad.

Dear Reader,

I'd like to thank you for choosing this book and for choosing to come along for Iggy's summer adventure (don't forget to pack sun cream!). I'd also like to take this opportunity to talk a little about the subject matter before we begin.

This book deals with the mental health condition Post Traumatic Stress Disorder, and specifically some of the symptoms this can present, such as flashbacks, anxious feelings and amnesia, as well as violence, homophobia and bullying. I think it's important to take a moment to acknowledge this before we dive in as these themes can often feel distressing to read about, fictional or otherwise.

Please know that this story is written with love and care, with the intention to shine light on authentic experiences in a safe way. I really hope you enjoy reading.

Daniel x

GAUDIUM IN VERITATE

ONE

I don't remember much about last summer.

Pops says I drowned and almost died. They found the body of a boy my age in the river after my accident and, with tears in his eyes, Pops told me that it so easily could have been me. That was enough for me to stop asking questions. It seemed the more I asked, the darker the answers became, and I hated seeing Pops so upset. But I'm still curious. I want to go back this year to do the same holiday again. For closure, I think, or to remember. I want to find the stuff I've lost. Navigating life with a head full of broken memories isn't all that cute. I want to retrace my steps, all the way back to the river if I can, because I want to know every last detail about why. Why did I jump into a river? A river known to be dangerous. A river that kills. I'm ready to face those darker answers. I want to. I think.

Does that sound weird?

I dunno, maybe this is me, Iggy Caddock, entering my 'weird girl' era.

'How has this week been?' asks Miss Steadman, my therapist. She's sitting directly opposite me, smiling.

'Fine,' I reply, which makes me feel stupid. I don't think the word 'fine' is very useful in a therapy session. 'Sorry, miss.'

'I'm not a teacher, Iggy.'

She has to remind me of this quite a lot. I'm supposed to call her by her first name, which is Sian, but I always forget.

'It's been easier this week . . . Sian.'

'Did the exercise I gave you for sleep help?' she asks.

'I think it did,' I say.

There's a peace lily in here with one white flower. There are prints of paintings by Monet and Lowry on the walls. I think the one in the corner is van Gogh, but it's nothing too stimulating. Stimulating would be counterproductive. There are neat cushions on two grey armchairs, facing each other, and a rug that screams Ikea. If this room had a flavour, it would be vanilla. I can taste it on my tongue, sickly sweet. It's actually making me feel a little nauseous.

'You say you haven't heard the noise *much*,' she continues, picking up on an earlier comment I made, because using my own words against me is a particular skill of hers. 'So tell me – what happens when you do hear it?'

I take a breath in through my nose and count to four. I hold it before I exhale, like she told me to. 'I feel, um . . . scared, I suppose.'

'Here, have a sip of water.'

She gestures, palm up, to the glass on the table beside me.

I pick it up and take a big gulp, and then I swallow hard, as if this will clear a path in my throat for my words to crawl through.

'I'm scared because I think it means I'm . . . crazy,' I say.

'Maybe we shouldn't use that word.'

Trust me to have a full repertoire of words never to be used in a therapy session. Talking to her is hard. I thought therapists were supposed to smile and nod, not pick apart your entire vocabulary.

I can think of no better word than 'crazy'. It's been with me for almost a whole year now. That's how long it's been since the summer that changed my life forever, the summer my joy decided to pack her bags and make a beeline for warmer climates, leaving me with overly cautious parents and on first-name terms with the school therapist.

'What are you thinking about?' she asks me.

My eye wanders over the bookshelf behind her, stopping on a Latin quote in a golden picture frame: *Gaudium in veritate*, which means 'joy in truth'. It's one of her favourites. I've been staring at it a lot lately. First comes truth, and then joy. That's what the quote means.

'Iggy?' she begins, tilting her head to one side.

'Sorry,' I say. 'I'm thinking that . . . I might be . . . permanently damaged?'

It's not a complete lie.

'Your scans showed no brain damage,' she says.

'I know,' I say. 'But sometimes I think I've tapped into some part of my consciousness that I wasn't supposed to tap into. You know? I've replaced my real memories with stuff that never happened. I've become this glitch in the matrix, and now I'm hearing things and seeing things that I know aren't there.'

'Seeing things?' she says. 'This is new.'

Her eyes light up because I've finally given her something to sink her teeth into, so her years of training, studying every one of the books that sit so neatly on the shelf behind her, can be put to good use. I can almost see her report already, written in red pen, because she always writes significant stuff in red, which in all honesty seems macabre. She's going to feed back to the powers-that-be, also known as my parents, that I'm seeing things, smiling as she writes every blood-coloured word.

Every week I come here, I remember for her sake that it's her job to make me talk about the stuff I don't want to. Talking means she can tick all of the relevant boxes and type up her reports accordingly. I guess these sessions have become farcical; I say what I think she wants to hear, she does the necessary paperwork and nothing ever changes. I never tell her what I'm really thinking because there's no easy way to talk about that stuff. But, at the same time, the plaster that's holding me together can't stick forever. It has to come off at some point because it's old and festering, peeling away from my skin at the edges, folding in and stuck thick with dirt. This plaster is no longer healing the wound beneath it, but making it worse. It's starting to smell. Bad. Time is running out.

'I think the *noise* is concerning me the most right now,' I say. 'Maybe we could get back to that?'

She raises her eyebrows and scribbles something in her notebook; probably something along the lines of 'cut me off rudely' or 'refused to talk' or 'raised their voice'; she's burnt me with those words before.

'OK,' she says, looking up. 'Tell me about that. When was the last time you heard it?'

I take another breath. I take another sip of water. 'Last week,' I whisper.

'Have you thought about what triggered it?' she asks.

'We're going away again.' I shrug.

'Back to the same place?' she asks.

Definitely. Probably. I think so.

My parents are both teachers, so they get a six-week break from work every year, meaning every summer we spend about a month touring Europe in our camper-van that spends the rest of the year parked on the drive, gathering fallen leaves and moss around its wheels.

But this year I'm the one who insisted we go. I'm the one who wanted this holiday. Pops and Dad had talked about a few weeks in Cornwall, but I told them that it has to be France. If you run from the monster it chases you, so you have to stand your ground; look it dead in the eye. France is where my monster lurks. France is where I'll find the truth of what happened that day. And so France it has to be.

'Do you think you're ready for this, Iggy?' she asks.

I don't know, I think.

But Cornwall just won't cut it. And what's the other option, staying home? If I stay home, Pops won't go either. And Dad won't go because he's useless without Pops. I already ruined my family's last summer break. I'm not going to ruin this one too.

I shake my head and cross my arms across my chest because I'm finding that talking, even though we're just skimming the surface, is making me feel nervous. This is my last session of the year before summer. This can't be the time I break, this can't be the time I reverse a whole year's worth of keeping myself together.

'Take another sip—' she begins.

'I . . . don't need another sip,' I say. I sound exasperated, strained even, like I'm lifting something heavy and I need to put it down.

The room falls into silence, an echo ringing off the back of my words.

'I think a few weeks in the sun will do you good,' she says eventually. 'I can see you're still experiencing symptoms of distress.'

'I'm . . . fine,' I whimper, keeping my eyes directed at the rug.

'Iggy . . . that word,' she says.

'OK – I'm feeling a little nervous, but, you're right – it's nothing a holiday can't fix. Is that better?'

When the session is over I head to the bathroom.

Once inside, I walk over to the sink, jamming the plug in the plughole and turning on both taps. I watch as the basin quickly fills, fresh water swilling and bubbling its way to the top, and then I shove my head in, gripping the porcelain edges until my knuckles turn the same white. The water splashes over my feet, shattering across the bathroom floor like glass. And I know I'm only making a mess. But sometimes I feel like I have to make mess. Sometimes I need this. I read somewhere that water has memory, which is why returning here, underwater, to the place my trauma lives, brings me the sort of relief that therapy sessions can't.

When I'm done I lift myself out slowly, peeking at my face in the mirror through long tendrils of wet hair.

'Gaudium in veritate,' I whisper.

Can it really be that simple?

TWO

Pops is standing in the kitchen, a map of the Mediterranean sprawled out in front of him, a random object on each of the four corners to stop it from curling in on itself: a bowl full of Mini Gems, a pepper mill, a pink salt lamp and an old doorknocker shaped like an elephant that used to hang on Granma's kitchen door.

'Hello, darling!' he says, removing his glasses. Every time I see Pops, whether I'm gone for a minute or a day, he greets me this way. His smile and arms are always wide open and his voice is full of sunshine. I feel very lucky to have a father like him. 'Have you had the most gorgeous day?'

'It's been all right,' I say, reaching forward and grabbing a handful of Mini Gems from the north-eastern corner of his map (Georgia, I think).

'I'm planning our route,' he says. 'Would you like to hear it?'

I nod.

We've been on the same sort of holiday for as long as I can remember. Sometimes we go south-west to Portugal, sometimes south-east – as far as Bulgaria once. There's usually a plan in place as all the good campsites get booked up super early, but there's room for spontaneity too.

On one occasion we found, quite by accident, the most

incredible campsite near the Pyrenees in Spain, where the view of the mountains was breathtaking, while on another, we spent the night in some random French service station where the view of a communal toilet wasn't *quite* as breathtaking. It's all part of the adventure. But this year it feels like there's no space for spontaneity, or even adventure, which makes me feel guilty.

I'm the one who asked for last year's holiday again.

'First stop-off is Rouen,' he says, tapping his finger off the map. 'It's where they burnt Joan of Arc. Look, I found this quote.' He passes me a white Post-it note with *Go forward bravely; fear nothing* written on it. 'I think it's fitting, don't you agree?'

It's almost as if he's not just passing me a Post-it, but some of Joan of Arc's strength too. He knows how much of a big deal this holiday is, and he's trying to lighten my load. Just having him make this sort of effort, having him care this much, makes me feel good.

'Then it's two whole weeks in Salon-de-Provence,' he continues. 'We're on the exact same campsite as last year. Then along the Riviera to Saint-Tropez and Nice, before crossing into Italy for Portofino.' He looks up from the map. 'I thought it might be nice to go a little further this year, so I thought Pisa and Rome before heading back through France all the way to ... Paris!' He taps his finger on the map. 'Thirty whole days of sunshine, culture and delicious food. Doesn't that sound delightful?'

I've never been to Rome before. I've never been to Paris either. Usually, the Family Caddock stays off the beaten track, keeping it rustic in random campsites and caravan parks throughout Europe. Pops is an art teacher in a high school, which means our holidays always include visits to galleries and museums. I don't think Dad cares all that much about them – he teaches science at the university – but he does care a great deal about Pops, so he's always happy to tag along. The galleries and museums we normally frequent are low-key, but by the sounds of this year's itinerary we'll be visiting some of the most famous ones in the world.

It's as if this summer is on steroids.

Pops walks around the breakfast bar and places a hand on my arm. 'It's going to be the best summer yet,' he says. 'I promise you, Iggy.'

He kisses my forehead, and I smile and nod, because he deserves a smile and nod. Last summer he stayed at my bedside the entire time. I was pretty out of it, but Dad told me later that he even slept at the hospital, and wouldn't so much as go to the bathroom unless someone was there to keep an eye on me. I don't remember much about the day I woke up in a French hospital, dazed and confused after an accident that almost cost me my life, but I do remember that his was the first face I saw when I did. His was the first face I needed to see too. It was because of him that I was able to take some comfort in the fact that I was OK when I could have so easily not been. It was because of him that I had every scan going, including a brain scan. Everything was fine. Well. Everything was fine physically, at least. I only wish they had a machine at the hospital that could assess my emotional damage. I wish they had a way of knowing how long I would feel so spaced out for.

If I'd known it would be nearing a year, maybe I could have done something about it.

Maybe.

I don't know.

Therapy was my parents' idea, their way of helping to take care of my mental state. I wish I'd made more progress this year but, I dunno, talking about things hasn't made much of a difference. And I know this is partly down to my reluctance to share, but that's just how it goes. Sian Steadman couldn't get it out of me, and so inside it stays in a place even I can't access. But I want to. I want to move on. I'm done with the mystery. I'm ready to face what happened last year and find my truth.

'And . . . Dijon?' I ask.

Pops looks up, concern sketching three strong lines across his forehead. 'There's an option to stay there on our way to Paris,' he mutters, looking down at the map.

Dijon is where my accident happened. I think both Pops and Dad were shocked when I asked to go back, especially since the only place any of us saw there was the hospital. But even they must realise that I need to know what happened; I need to know why I did what I did. It blows my mind that I was so careless, especially when I know water so well. I've been swimming for as long as I can remember and I'm definitely the strongest in my class. I know about rip currents, and I know that a fast-moving river is never a good idea.

'I'd like to go,' I say.

'I know,' he says. 'And I think that's brave of you, poppet, but we'll see how you feel closer to the time. There are a hundred towns in France we can stop at if we need to – I've actually been fancying Annecy for a while; its old town looks beautiful, with a chateau that once homed the Count of Geneva.' He drops his head towards the map again. 'Your bag is already laid out on your bed,' he says. 'I'm making salade Niçoise for tea tonight. We'll be eating the real authentic stuff soon enough, in a quaint little bistro in Marseille, I imagine.' He grips his hands into fists, shaking them at his sides like that excited-face emoji, and then he begins to flounce around the kitchen, opening cupboards and drawers, gathering the utensils he needs to make our last family meal before the holiday. 'Oh, I forgot to say,' he says over his shoulder as he reaches into the fridge for a bag of tomatoes. 'The Redwoods are already at the campsite in Provence. Julie's school broke up early, so they arrived this morning. Isn't that just perfect? There'll be some familiar faces waiting for us when we get there!'

I stop in the middle of the kitchen; the faint excitement I'd started to feel fading at the edges because holidaying with the Redwoods again means only one thing.

'Is *he* going to be with us *all* summer?' I ask.

'If you mean Evan,' Pops begins, 'then, yes – of course. Julie and I have planned our routes out together, so we'll be seeing a lot of them again this year. Doesn't that sound fun?'

Pops and Dad made friends with Julie and Dave Redwood on a campsite in Spain when I was eleven. To my parents it felt like destiny that we would find a family that was the same size as ours, with kids the same age as their own, parents who both worked in schools, and who owned a camper-van and therefore enjoyed the same sort of holidays as us. It was just expected that Evan and I would become best friends and everything would be so perfect. And I guess it would have gone down like that had Evan Redwood not been the very worst person to ever walk the earth.

I can't believe it's been a whole blissful year since I've been forced to spend time with the person who so affectionately refers to me as Biggy Iggy because of my size. Yeah. That's the level of idiotship we're dealing with, people.

'I'm not hanging out with him,' I say. 'You can't force me this year – I'm sixteen years old. I'm an adult.'

'Technically speaking – you're not,' he says.

'You can't make me!' I say.

He stops chopping and turns to face me, a serious look in his eyes. 'Nobody is forcing you to do anything you don't want to, Iggy,' he says. 'Although . . . Evan is such a nice boy, from such a lovely family, I can't see why the two of you can't get along.'

I can, I think.

If I listed all of the mean things he's said and done to me over the years, including calling me names, water-bombing me in the pool and whacking me in the face with a tennis ball so my lip swelled up to three times its usual size, I'm sure Pops wouldn't be waving the Evan flag so obviously in my face right now. I'm almost grateful for the memory loss; at least it means I have one less summer spent with him to remember. *Every cloud*, I think.

'I'm starting to have second thoughts about this holiday,' I mutter.

'Oh, don't be silly,' says Pops, wafting away my sarcasm. 'It's going to be wonderful. Please don't leave it too late to pack. We have an early start in the morning.'

I begin to shuffle reluctantly out of the kitchen, making lots of loud, unenthusiastic noises so Pops can hear. This is partly for dramatic effect, but also because I would like him to take my concerns about Evan seriously. There's a reason why keeping away from him is so much more important this year than any of the others that came before. I don't know why, maybe it's because I'm standing in the kitchen right now, but when I think of him I can taste potato salad, thick and creamy and cold. It's the weirdest sensation. I get this strange feeling too, sort of like sadness and anger smashed together. It burns away somewhere on my insides, momentarily stopping me in my tracks by the kitchen door.

'Evan Redwood and I will *never* be friends,' I mutter, before turning my back and walking out.

THIS SUMMER

THREE

We stop off twice in France on our way to the south, with one night in Rouen, and another just outside a town called Brive-la-Gaillarde. It's actually nice to spend a couple of nights just the three of us. Our holidays are always filled with so many people, and I don't always love being in a crowd. It's great to start this way, dipping my toes into summer before the madness begins. Being able to sit around our foldaway picnic table, a citronella candle burning away in the middle to deter unwanted mosquitos, with Dad and Pops, just talking and listening to cricket song as it fills the darkness feels so good. I didn't realise just how much I've missed this. I become something else when I'm so far away from home, free of the routines that bind me. I become a wild thing when my excitement overpowers the ordinary. How could I forget about this feeling? It seems so big now.

After a quiet night on the campsite in Brive, we hit the road early and make good time on our arrival into Salon-de-Provence.

The campsite is huge. Our pitch is a little way from the excitement of the main area, where there are pools, bars and restaurants. We drive slowly past caravans and tents and wooden chalets, and basketball and tennis courts, and a golf course. The whispers of last summer grow louder; I remember this place, and how excited we were when we arrived. It's probably the biggest campsite we've ever stayed on, more like a small town, enclosed from the outside world by a tall, white-painted railing that runs around the border.

As we turn on to the road that leads us to our pitch, I notice the blue and brown stripes of the Redwood camper-van. They're here, and we're here, and so summer can officially begin. A small part of me is already missing the gentle tranquillity of the night before, when I had Dad and Pops to myself and didn't feel like I needed to be anything: enthusiastic, sociable, on guard. I don't know, I guess I don't want to force anything, to be anything that I'm not, but I suppose it's inevitable when faced with someone you don't like.

'You made it!' says Dave Redwood, an upbeat man with big blue eyes and ruddy, sunburnt cheeks. I always think of him as looking like a giant garden gnome. I smile back through the camper-van window. Pops was right; it's nice to be welcomed by a familiar face. I'm glad he's the first Redwood family member we've seen.

'Just about,' says Pops, opening the passenger door and jumping out.

He and Dave help Dad manoeuvre his way into the plot, and as soon as he stops the engine, he folds forwards over the steering wheel as if deflating. It's been a long drive today – we've been going for around five hours.

Pops opens the side door from outside, and I unfasten my seat belt and step out. It's hot, even in the shade.

'Hey, Iggy,' says Dave Redwood. 'How's it going?'

'It's going good,' I say.

'Glad to hear it,' he says. 'Evan's around here somewhere. I know he's been looking forward to seeing you.'

I had a lot of time to think on the journey down here about my approach to Evan this year. I've decided that, as this summer is an important one, I'm not going to get into all of that. As soon as I see him I'm going to nip the childish banter in the bud, no questions asked. He doesn't like me, and I don't like him, and it's perfectly acceptable to keep out of each other's way this year. There's no point making this difficult or awkward for anybody. We're both nearing adulthood, and I'm prepared to act like it.

My only hope is that he is too.

From my place in the shade, I notice a guy walking down the road towards us, towards me, smiling with those TV-presenter sort of teeth. You know the ones: super white and shiny. I don't know him, so I look around to see if there's anybody else standing behind me. But it's just me he's staring at, and I mean *really* staring.

'Hey, Iggy,' he says, when he's within earshot.

I do a quick double take. He's kinda attractive, with a defined brow, thick eyebrows and a blond beard. He's wearing all of these cool bands on his wrists, and he has a bandana tied around his shoulder-length sandy-coloured hair to keep it away from his face, but his eyes are the same shade of blue they've always been.

No. It can't be.

'Oh, there you are, Evan,' says Dave, smiling at the boy in front of me. 'Look who's arrived!'

Evan Redwood?

The brat I spent past summers with was shaven-headed (and wildly irritating). There was no beard. There was no sandy hair, or wristbands, or bandana. The Evan Redwood I know is all hard edges and sportswear. This guy isn't any of these things. He's barefoot, and bearded, and bohemian. I squint my eyes to take a closer look. I recognise the nose. I think. And he always had nice eyes; I was able to appreciate that even when he was being beastly towards me. But that's where the similarities between the guy standing in front of me and the guy who used to kick over my sandcastles end.

'How was the journey down?' he asks.

'*Shit*,' I say, without meaning to.

'Oh no,' he says. 'I'm sorry to hear that.'

'No, I didn't mean the journey,' I whisper. 'I meant you.'

'I'm shit?' he asks.

Even his voice has changed. Where before it was high-pitched and sharp, his laughter able to cut into my skin like barbed wire, it's now mellow, deep and warm.

'No,' I say. 'That's not what I meant.'

Although it kind of is, because of all the tricks he could pull on me this year, this has to be the worst. Doesn't it? The guy I dislike most in the world suddenly looking like a YouTube star was not on my summer bingo card. So, yeah, he's a bit of a shit.

'Hi, Evan,' says Pops, walking over to us. 'It's so lovely to see you. Isn't it lovely to see him, Iggy?'

I nod. Weakly.

'Were you just at the pool?' asks Pops.

'Yeah,' says Evan. 'I was with some of the guys, but I saw your van driving past the main house and thought I'd come and say hi.'

'So thoughtful of you,' says Pops. 'Isn't that thoughtful of him, Iggy?'

Pops is *really* making an effort, putting on this phony voice that makes him sound like a children's TV presenter. It's equally confusing and cringe at the same time.

He turns back to the camper-van, so he can get on with setting up our pitch; folding out the picnic table, pulling out the canopy and stringing fairy lights between the van and the posts either side. I just stand here. Staring at him.

'Do you want to come to the pool while your folks set up?' he asks.

'No,' I say.

'You sure?' he asks. 'There's a group of us that have been hanging out for the past few days. I can introduce you to everyone.'

As he reels off a list of names of people I have no intention of talking to, I start to grow suspicious. This whole new image thing seems a little *too* extreme.

'You look . . . different,' I say, cutting him off.

He nods. 'I *am* different,' he says.

He seems sincere, but to the point where it isn't sincere any more, but something forced and fake. Which I guess means that, actually, he's insincere . . . to the point of nausea.

'*Why?*' I whisper, and it's partly to myself.

'I guess,' he begins, 'well – I had to change . . . after what happened.'

'What happened?' I ask.

In this moment I get a glimpse of the old Evan, because he looks as if he's about to laugh. I expect to hear the sharp, stabbing sound and to feel embarrassment and frustration bubbling up inside me as the same old Evan Redwood treats me like I'm nothing but a joke. I instinctively step back from him, crossing my arms across my chest, every muscle in my body tensing as if bracing for impact. But then something strange happens. His eyes begin to change shape, the emotion behind them shifting to something much darker.

'But . . .' he begins, his lips tight and pursed. 'How do you not . . . Wait, you don't . . . ?'

'I don't *what*?' I ask.

His mouth hangs open. Clearly, he expects me to remember something. Didn't he get the memo?

'*Hi, Iggy*,' someone sings.

In the corner of my eye I see the purple bikini top and tangerine sarong of Julie Redwood approaching. She throws her arms around me, the smell of coconut-scented sun cream and sweet perfume distracting me for a moment.

'You look so well,' she says. 'Don't they look well, Evan?'

He nods.

'It's so lovely to be back together again,' says Julie. 'It really feels like summer now. Look at you both – my babies, all grown up.' She wipes an imaginary tear from her eye.

'Is that Julie?' I hear Pops say as he emerges from the camper-van.

'Hello, darling!' she says, throwing her arms out. She walks towards him, taking her bright colours, sweet smells and noise with her, leaving me alone with Evan again.

He's still looking at me; the same faraway look in his eye.

'I need to unpack,' I say, pointing over my shoulder.

'OK,' he says. 'I guess I'll . . . see you later?'

But I don't answer him. I just turn my back and walk away. I don't need to unpack; unpacking can wait. I just really need to get out of his way, really need a minute to process what's going on. I was prepared for confrontation, and humiliation, and all of the other things the old Evan brought to the table. But this?

Why do I feel like I'm being pranked right now?

We all head to the rotisserie place on the hill outside the campsite for dinner, like one big dysfunctional family. The mouth-watering smell of roasting chicken floats towards me as we ascend the dirt track towards the restaurant. From outside it doesn't look like much, but the food is so good. It's probably the best chicken and chips I've ever tasted. Afterwards, we make a pit stop at the bar at the other end of the campsite, because there's a flamenco dancer performing tonight and Pops is a huge fan of ballroom dancing. Dad got him lessons last Christmas and they've been going once a week ever since.

'Doesn't Evan look different this year?' asks Pops as we walk behind the Redwoods into the bar. 'Jules was saying he's into his fitness – especially outdoorsy stuff, like rock climbing and kayaking. She said he's keen to find somewhere to do it while we're away. He'd love it if you could join him.'

'Not going to happen,' I mutter under my breath.

I've never been a rock-climbing type of gal and I can see no reason to start now.

'A month is a long time to hold a grudge,' says Dad.

'He's not going anywhere, Iggy,' Pops says. 'And we're all here to have a nice time. A lot of effort, not to mention money, has gone into this holiday, and I'd like you to think about that before you start all of this up again.'

'Start all of *what* up again?' I snap.

'I'm just saying,' he says. 'Find a way to move on, for all our sakes. Is this really the hill you want to die on?'

Why am I suddenly being made to feel like I'm overreacting? Evan has done horrible things in the past. The bust lip and name-calling aside, my instinct tells me there might even be other reasons to dislike him this year. I don't know how to describe the feeling; it's like I have this *sense* of something.

Are my parents right; should I just forgive and forget? I don't think so. He may have everybody else fooled, but I'm not buying this new version of Evan without asking a few questions first.

'I'm going back,' I say, before we've reached the table.

'Oh, come on, Iggy,' says Pops.

'I want an early night,' I say. It's too much for me to sit around playing happy families with him. It just feels wrong. 'It's been a long day.'

Pops looks at Dad, who then shrugs in response. 'Are you sure you don't want to watch the show?' he asks. 'Senorita Margarita is supposed to be a fabulous dancer – world-class, I hear.'

'I'm good,' I say. 'I want to be fresh for my first proper day here.'

Dad pulls me closer and kisses my forehead. 'OK, my darling,' he says. 'Do you want us to come with you?'

'No, stay and enjoy the show,' I say. 'I'll see you in the morning. We said the beach tomorrow, right?'

'We did,' says Pops excitedly. 'But not too early – we're all tired after so much travelling.'

They join the Redwoods at a table near the stage, and I make my way through cocktail umbrellas and Hawaiian shirts towards the door. But before I reach it, I hear a voice call me back.

'Hey, Iggy!' I turn to see Evan walking towards me. 'Are you leaving?'

I nod. I find that I'm strangely shy around this version of him. I don't trust him, any more than I used to, and I'm so bad with all the fakery. Seriously. I'm like an open book. My face always shows exactly how I'm feeling. If this really is the new him, then I'm going to need a minute to adjust.

'Didn't you fancy the show?' he asks.

'I'm tired,' I say.

He purses his lips. 'That's understandable. Hey – what are you up to tomorrow?'

'Just heading to the beach with my parents,' I mumble.

'Oh. Right.'

He doesn't look as if he's going to say anything else, and so I take this opportunity to make my escape. But then . . .

'I can walk you back, if you like?' he says, appearing at my side.

Wait. What is he doing? 'I'm OK,' I say.

'It's a big campsite, and you might get lost or—'

'Really, Evan,' I snap. 'I don't need you to walk me back.

I don't need you to do anything. I'm perfectly capable of finding the camper-van on my own.'

'Iggy—'

'Just . . . leave me,' I say, raising my hands. 'I'm tired and it's been a long day and I want to go back on my own. OK?'

I don't want to be this person, not when summer's just begun. And I feel bad for snapping at him, and that screws with my head a little because he's *Evan Redwood*. Snapping is nothing compared to the stuff he's done to me over the years. But still, I do, because snapping at someone is never OK. I think about apologising; he looks upset, but I don't want the conversation to start up again, and, even more than that, I don't want him to walk me back to the camper-van, so I decide it's for the best that I leave.

As I walk away, I begin to think about how blisteringly obvious it is that there's something going on with him this year. It hadn't occurred to me before; I guess I was still in shock, but now I'm beginning to wonder what's behind the image overhaul. It would seem that he's gone on some sort of personal journey, which in some ways I'm here for; I mean, who wants to stay a cretin forever? But in other ways I find this so suspicious, because the guy I knew would never, the guy I knew didn't have the capacity. And yet here he is, a whole new person.

I guess I underestimated him.

Which makes me wonder what else Evan Redwood might be capable of.

FOUR

There's a coach from the campsite that takes us to the beach. Pops has packed a freezer bag with enough food for the day, and we have a windbreak and an umbrella too. I have my paddleboard with me, so when the coach arrives I slide it into the hold with the rest of the bigger items. It'll just be the three of us today. The Redwoods have gone on an excursion to Marseille. We're going there in a couple of days, which means I have an Evan-free day until at least this evening. I can't think of a better way to officially start the holiday.

As we pull on to the main road, turning past the gatehouse and then through the pine trees, I think about how familiar this seems. I remember this coach. I remember the campsite's tall gates and the pine trees growing either side. I remember the peach orchard next door and the sunflower fields opposite, and all of the quaint French houses with their painted shutters and balustrades.

But it's when I see the sun shining on to the Mediterranean Sea for the first time this year that I begin to really remember the way summer makes me feel.

'Isn't this simply heavenly?' asks Pops, as we make our way across fine white sand to find the perfect spot, which isn't too far away from the water.

We set up camp at the far end of the beach, Dad hammering the windbreak into the sand with his sandal – even though there's no wind at all – and Pops laying out towels and sun cream and his stack of summer reads. I dump my yellow rucksack on to the sand. I love this bag, it reminds me of summer too. I don't know why I never use it throughout the rest of the year, because it's the perfect size, with a compartment for my iPad at the back, and tons of pockets. I shove my hand into one and find something hard and grooved. I grip it with my fingertips and pull it out, a white seashell, all spiralling and pointy. I hold it up, its smooth enamelled surface shining in the sunlight. This shell reminds me of all the beach days that came before this one, like the one when Dad took a picture of me sitting on a rock with waves spraying up behind me, like in *The Little Mermaid*. It took us ages to get the perfect image. It made for some amusing outtakes though. Or the time Pops bought a giant inflatable shell and an unexpected storm hit and it blew away.

'Are you going in, Iggs?' asks Dad.

I look out to sea, at the hugeness of it, and my belly fills with butterflies, dragonflies and hummingbirds.

'You don't have to if you don't want to,' says Pops.

'No, I . . . want to,' I say, gripping the shell in my hand. I have such fond memories of snorkelling and paddleboarding, and I'm not done making them. The sea has always played such an important part in our family holidays, and I don't want things to change all because of a silly mistake I made last year. 'I wouldn't have brought the paddleboard if I didn't.'

'Just dip your toes in,' says Pops. 'You don't have to take the board in today.'

'I want to,' I say. *Actually, I have to*, I think, because if I back out now then I might never do it.

So I shove the shell back in my bag and then make my way to the water's edge, paddleboard tucked under my arm. I'm a strong swimmer and there are plenty of lifeguards on this beach, and the sea looks calm today and I'll be fine. The end.

Pops follows me to the water and sits in the shallows, stretching out his legs and leaning back so he can tilt his head up to the sun like a sunflower. I place my paddleboard on to the surface and wade in until I'm up to my waist. The sea is warm and so clear; a school of tiny silver fish flit past me, their scales catching the sun like sequins when they change direction. I glide my hands through, pushing the water around me. This doesn't feel so bad, and there's certainly no reason to be afraid.

I place my hands on top of my paddleboard and slide on belly-first. Then I swing my legs around until I'm straddling it, facing inland. Pops gives me an 'OK' sign with his right hand. I mimic him to show him that I am. I'm perfectly OK. Actually, I'm more than OK because this feels so freeing. I thought being in the water would awaken some repressed fear in me, but as I float here, gently bobbing up and down, up and down, I can feel the heaviness I've been carrying around since last summer begin to sail away. It's as if it can't exist here in the water. Here, even the heaviest things float.

I turn my board around so I'm facing the horizon, at the perfect line between blue sky and sea, and then I begin to paddle.

And it's . . . just like it was. Each scoop of my paddle propels me forward, and for the first time in a year I feel like I'm in control. My head feels so clear, the things I thought I'd lost becoming ever more visible, like seeing right to the bottom. Who knew paddleboarding could make me feel like *this*?

I decide to be braver still and come up on to my knees, and then I stand slowly, distributing my weight between each foot to steady myself. It's even better than I remember. As I move across the undulating surface, the glass-bell-sound of water ringing all around me, I begin to remember. I see myself learning to swim with Dad. I see myself collecting shells, riding a pedalo, and paddleboarding just like I am now. I see myself swimming with a turtle, its dark eyes moving towards me through greenish-blue water before it swoops to deeper depths. I see myself in my coral-coloured swimming shorts, the ones I wore for, like, three summers in a row, before I started wearing a bikini top, before I asked my family to start calling me Iggy.

Instead of breaking me, it feels like the water is gently putting me back together again. Maybe water really does hold memory after all, because the Mediterranean Sea seems to have kept so many of mine.

I close my eyes, tilting my head towards the sky so I can sink deeper into this feeling, a feeling that had I known its importance I would never have misplaced, when my board bumps into something and I lose my balance. I try to stay upright on my own, but the board is wobbling way too much. I feel a warm hand grab my arm as someone tries to help me. But my wet skin is too slippery, and I tumble headfirst into the sea.

Summer disappears as I fall into silence; the first proper quiet I've heard in a year. It's like there's nothing else. The sea is cool and calm and way bigger than me, and all I can do is surrender to it. I should feel scared. I know I should after last year and everything that's happened since. But it feels good to surrender. Feels good to let go.

When I push through the surface, I see a guy straddling his paddleboard next to mine.

'Are you OK?' he asks. 'I'm so sorry – who even does that? I'm so clumsy on this thing.'

'I'm fine,' I say, pushing myself back on to my board.

'It's my first time out with the new board,' he says. 'It's taking some getting used to. I didn't mean to push you in.'

'It's honestly fine,' I say. 'No harm done.' *This time*, I think morbidly, then shove the thought to the back of my mind.

I spin myself round so I'm straddling the board again, and then grab my paddle, raising it high so I can plunge it into the water and continue my adventure.

'Leaving already?' he asks.

This forces me to stop, forces me to look at him. Properly. He's surprisingly handsome, with delicate facial features and green eyes, but in an I-don't-give-a-damn-about-it sort of way. His long hair is tied back with a tartan scrunchie and he has at least three facial piercings.

'Is there more?' I ask.

'I hope so,' he says. 'I hope I won't forever be remembered as the guy who knocked you off your board.'

A shallow laugh escapes me. 'Knocked me off my board? You make it sound so romantic.'

He smiles; he doesn't chuckle or laugh dismissively, he *smiles*. It catches me off guard because in this moment a smile means something. I bite my lower lip as I look away. Wait. Why is my heart racing?

'I'm Roscoe, by the way,' he says. 'And you're . . . Iggy?'

'Do I know you?' I ask sharply, because if this guy turns out to be another cretin from previous summers who's undergone a serious makeover I might flip my lid.

'I saw you talking to some guy at the main house last night,' he says, shaking his head. 'I heard him call you Iggy, and thought it was a cute name.'

He smiles again, and it seems to say so many things. It says: *You're safe with me. You can talk to me. I'm not like Evan Redwood. I'm nothing like him.* It's weird that a smile can say all of that. I'm suddenly thrown into panic mode. Is he flirting with me? Is a hot guy blatantly flirting with me on my very first day of summer? I don't know if I dare believe it.

But he's still smiling, and I think he might be.

'Yeah, that was me,' I say, channelling my nervous energy into tucking a loose hair behind my ear.

'Phew!' he says, pretending to wipe his brow with his fingertips. 'That could have been awkward.'

He presses his lips together as he glances back to shore, and I allow my eyes a moment to wander across his face, drinking more of him in: his freckles, his eyelashes, his dimples. So a handsome guy who thinks my name is cute is flirting with me. And, just to make this moment even more extra, he's staying at the same campsite? What is happening right now? Is the universe finally paying out after all my hours of suffering?

'Did you just arrive, or . . . ?' I ask.

'Only yesterday,' he says. He's British, which means his school must have broken up this week too, although I can't quite place his accent. 'We have two weeks at the campsite, and then we're travelling across the south of France. I have family in Saint-Tropez, so we go every year.'

Two weeks, which is the same as me. And we're going to Saint-Tropez too. I'm pretty sure Pops mentioned it when he told me the itinerary. I don't know if it's the first-time-being-flirted-with-in-a-long-time excitement or not, but without me telling it to, my mind starts playing a summer montage in which Roscoe features *heavily*.

'Where do you hang out at the campsite?' I ask, because seeking him out again might have just shot to the top of my priority list.

'Depends,' he shrugs. 'I don't know my way around yet. Have you been before?'

Telling Roscoe that we came to the campsite last year doesn't feel like a wise move. It would mean explaining why I can't remember anything about it, and I don't want to muddy what feels like an unexpectedly perfect moment. So I say, 'When I was younger. It's changed a lot.'

'People tend to hang out around the main house, I think,' he continues. 'But I like to do my own thing. I'm excited to explore a little more.'

I can tell right away that he isn't like anybody else. The way he presents himself, the way he talks and smiles and moves, he's *my* kind of different. Also, he doesn't want to hang around the main house, which means he won't be one of Evan

Redwood's 'guys' this year, which means we can absolutely, one hundred per cent be friends. Although I'm thinking that 'friends' might not cut it.

I take a moment to imagine how it would feel to be with Roscoe this summer. It's taken me coming back here to realise it, but I'm a different Iggy when I'm on holiday. I'm not a person who's tied to their past mistakes – or, more specifically, *mistake*. Actually, I don't even have to think about that. As far as Roscoe is concerned, the accident last year never happened. I can be free of it, as easy as surrendering to the sea. I can be Iggy again, who loves to swim, and hang out, and bump into cute strangers on their paddleboards. It hadn't occurred to me before now, but it seems totally possible that this summer I could start again. Why didn't I think of this sooner?

I'm not the best at asking for what I want, so I say, 'I'd like to explore a little more too,' and hope he gets the hint.

I wait, watching his sunlit face, trying to make sense of his expression, because if I've misjudged the flirt situation this moment could switch from romance to tragedy with revolting speed. Why is he taking so long to respond?

'Maybe we could . . . explore together?' he says.

Bingo.

'I'd like that,' I say.

'How about tonight?' he asks. 'I could meet you by the tennis courts at eight?'

'OK,' I say, some fragile part of me growing surer, stronger.

'Awesome!' he says.

He tries to climb up to standing on his board again, but

quickly loses his footing and falls forward, which makes me laugh.

'I'm sorry,' I say. 'I don't mean to . . . You need to hold your centre more.'

'My what?' he asks.

'Like, tense your belly when you stand,' I say. And I don't know what confident main-character energy possesses me, but I lean forward and press my hand against his stomach. I don't expect it to be so hard and warm. I don't expect to feel a spark where I've touched him either. But I do. 'It'll make it easier,' I whisper, as our eyes meet.

He tries again. He falls again. This time we both laugh.

'I need to get the hang of the bigger board,' he begins. 'I can't spend the entire summer banging into unsuspecting people with cute names.'

I bite my bottom lip again to stop my smile from spreading too widely across my face. It always means so much to me that people like the name I've chosen for myself. It feels even nicer coming from him.

He pushes himself on to his knees and then slowly stands, this time making it all the way.

'You did it!' I say, applauding him.

He goes to take a bow and his board wobbles. 'Whoa!' he says. 'I'm a menace on this thing.'

'You'll get the hang of it,' I say. 'The trick is to stay as still as possible.'

'Got it,' he says. He dips his paddle into the water and begins to move away. 'I'm doing it!' he says. 'Look at me – I'm doing it!'

'You *so* are,' I shout after him. 'Keep going.'

'No choice,' he says. 'I'll see you later, Iggy – if I can stop this thing!'

When I get back to the shallows, Pops is waiting for me at the water's edge.

'How was it?' he asks.

'It was really great,' I say, hopping off my board and dragging it on to the sand. 'Better than I remember, actually.'

'I'm so pleased!' he says. 'See, there was no need to be so worried after all, was there?'

'Um, was *I* worried? Or was that . . . ?'

'OK,' he says, holding up his hands. 'Maybe I was even more worried, but look how well you did. I'm so proud of you, Iggy. Truly.'

I walk back across the sand towards our spot, where Dad is sitting in the shade, earbuds in, watching something on his phone. He holds his thumbs up when he sees me, a questioning look across his face. I return the gesture, which makes him sink a little deeper into his sunbed. Dad might seem more laidback than Pops, but maybe we were all nervous about today.

I sit down on the towel next to my yellow bag and spray sun cream across my shoulders. As I rub the sweet-scented lotion into my warm skin, I think about the guy I just met. Roscoe. I don't think I've ever felt so comfortable around somebody so quickly. He even made me laugh, which never happens. I'm so sure he was flirting. It'd be so cringe if I've read this wrong. But there was definitely something there. Wasn't there?

'So what's the smile about?' asks Pops, taking a seat on his sun lounger.

'Nothing,' I say.

He tilts his head to one side because he's my dad and can see right through me, as easy as seeing through water.

'I've just . . .' I continue, 'I've decided, I think I want to start over – to not let what happened last year play such a big role this summer. Yeah. I think that's what I'm going to do.'

Pops sits up a little taller and lowers his sunglasses so I can see into his eyes.

'Well,' he begins. 'That certainly sounds like something to smile about.'

FIVE

I'm leaving the campsite shower block later that day; my freshly washed hair cleansed of sea salt and twisted up on top of my head, when I bump – literally – into Evan Redwood.

'Oh, sorry,' I say, dropping my wash bag. What is it with me and bumping into guys today?

'Oh, there you are,' he says, picking it up and handing it to me. I grip it tighter to my stomach, as if it can hide some part of me. I haven't forgotten the names he used to call me. 'Where have you been hiding?'

'Hiding?' I say defensively.

'I thought you'd be sitting out with your parents,' he says. 'We're just about to start a poker game with the cards I got from Marseille.'

Firstly, it's strange that he's noticed my absence. He's never taken any notice of me before. And secondly, which ties in with the first point – why would he care? Evan Redwood doesn't care if I miss out on poker games. He doesn't care if I miss out on anything.

'I was just showering,' I say.

'How was the beach?' he asks. 'Did you take your paddleboard? I know how much you like boarding.'

'Yeah, it was good,' I say.

'Excellent. So are you going to come and play?'

'Oh, I'm . . . Well, no – not tonight. I . . . have other plans this evening.'

'Plans? With who?'

He looks confused, like 'why would anybody refuse such an offer' sort of thing. But there's no way I'm letting Evan Redwood know my business. This is non-negotiable. Him knowing where I'm going and, more importantly, who I'm seeing, would turn a heart-skipping, stomach-flipping situation into something awkward and embarrassing.

'Just some girls I met at the beach,' I lie.

His face begins to twist in ways I've never seen it before. He moves from confused to hurt in two fluid facial expressions, like he's genuinely upset that I don't want to join in his poker game. He used to be so hyper and bubbly, sometimes he would stammer because he had so much to say. But now he's just sort of mumbling slowly as he pads from foot to foot. Like, seriously – who dis? I first thought the change in Evan had something to do with me; I thought he was forcing himself to be nice to me after what happened last year, probably at the request of his parents, but as I look into his face I get the feeling there's something else, and this isn't about me at all. Is Evan going through something?

'Are you OK?' I ask.

'Why wouldn't I be?' he responds.

'You just seem so . . . *changed*.' I'm choosing my words wisely because I don't want to offend him; a courtesy he's never afforded me before, I know, but I feel like I need to be gentler with him. I guess our old sparring days really are over, which I'm glad about because who has the energy? Don't get me wrong – I don't see a reconciliation on the cards, that isn't what I want, but being a little more caring towards him makes me realise I've been holding on to something that has ultimately done more damage to me than him. Maybe it's time I let it go? I really didn't see summer going this way, and look, we don't need to be friends, but we don't need to be enemies either.

'Has something happened?' I ask.

He begins to chew the side of his mouth, and I can see he's desperate to answer. But no words come. He just stares, his mouth pressing and twisting, and I can actually feel my pulse increasing it's that awkward.

'Forget I asked,' I say.

I go to walk past him, keeping my head down as I hurry towards the camper-van, but then he turns around and says, 'I *will* tell you. When the time is right – I'll tell you everything.'

Then he heads into the shower block, leaving me standing in the middle of the path feeling more confused than ever.

Roscoe is already waiting for me by the tennis courts.

I keep to the side of the road so he can't see me just yet. I want to take all of him in, his style, his hair, everything. He's all silver rings and Doc Martens, and he's wearing a black Dungeons & Dragons T-shirt even though it's summertime and most people are dressed in bright colours. He has a gingham shirt tied around his waist, and his hair is carefully tucked behind his ears. But it's his smile that outshines everything else. When he sees me his face lights up and it hits me somewhere low down.

'Iggy!' he says, pushing himself off the fence. 'Hey!'

'Hi,' I say, crossing the road.

I'm glad we get to meet this way, away from the crowds. I have this inexplicable need to find out more about him and meeting here, at the quiet end of the campsite, means we get to focus on each other without distractions. He seems so unlike any other guy, not only by the way he dresses but the way he looks at me, talks to me, smiles at me. Most guys tend to look me over, or try to 'figure me out'. Their words, not mine. I guess, because I don't conform to gender norms, making new connections with guys can be tricky, and, really, it's not something that bothers me. If by living my most authentic life I confuse ninety-nine per cent of guys then I'm OK with that. It makes finding that one per cent all the more meaningful.

'You look cute,' he says.

He's officially giving me 'one per cent' vibes. 'Sorry,' I say, chuckling to myself. 'Thanks. So do you.'

'Is that funny?' he asks.

'No. It's not. I'm just . . . I'm not used to being called that. I don't know why I laughed.' *Maybe because it feels nice?* 'How was the rest of your day? Did you get the hang of the paddleboard in the end?'

'Not really,' he says. 'My new board is way bigger so it's taking some getting used to. You're so good though. Have you been doing it for a while?'

'Every summer since I was, like, ten?' I shrug. 'It definitely gets easier. I wasn't sure if I could . . .' *do it again after last year.* I keep the second half of the sentence inside my head, because Roscoe doesn't need to know about that.

'Wasn't sure if you could . . . ?' he prompts.

'It's just been a while since I last used my board,' I say, trying my best to keep it cute. 'Turns out it's just like riding a bike.'

A car moves slowly down the road, and I step nearer to the railing to get out of its way. As I move closer to him, I get this warm feeling, prickling against my arms, causing the hairs to stand on end. I chance a quick look at him as he watches the car roll to the end of the track. That face. It's a work of angles, shadows and symmetry. It's sort of perfect, actually.

'I wish I could say the same,' he says. 'I'm great on a bike.'

'I'm a water baby,' I say. 'I got the board for Christmas one year. It was my favourite present ever.'

'So I'm guessing you're a strong swimmer?' he asks.

His question triggers a response somewhere in my head, somewhere behind my eyes, somewhere in the dark. I see a red sky, burning through criss-crossing branches, but they're distorted as if I'm seeing them through frosted glass, seeing them through water. I want to move towards them, I want to see them clearly, but I'm being pulled in the opposite direction, pulled down to darker places.

'Yeah . . . I guess so,' I say, shaking away the vision.

'What was that?' he asks.

'Nothing,' I say. 'I just remembered something. It's weird how being back in the same place can do that.'

'Oh, yeah – you've been here before, haven't you? You'll be able to show me round then.'

'I wouldn't be so sure,' I whisper.

'Which way should we go first?' he asks, pointing fingers in different directions. 'The main house is that way, so why don't we try *this* way?' He points to the opposite end of the road. Our pitch is in that direction, and I don't fancy walking past everyone as they sit outside the camper-van playing card games. That would be so awkward.

'How about we go straight ahead?' I ask. 'There's a park in the middle of the campsite, I think.'

'Lead the way.'

We walk alongside the tennis courts and then make a left turn deeper into the campsite, following our noses all the way to a pizza restaurant, which sits in a clearing by a gated play park. The smell of fresh bread, melting mozzarella and oregano makes my mouth water. Pizza is life and so I'd love a slice, but it's heaving in there, with a queue of people standing by the plinth outside, and I think we're trying to avoid crowds, so we settle for the park instead.

'Tell me something about you, Iggy,' he says, as I take a seat on one of the swings and he leans against the frame. 'What are your dreams and aspirations?'

It's thrilling to have this much of his attention. I feel as if that TikTok guy, the one who asks random people if he can paint their likeness while he questions them about life, has stopped me in the street. His green-eyed gaze is intense, moving over every part of me, but I don't feel self-conscious. I actually want him to see all of me, all of my curves and grooves and freckles. I want Roscoe to paint an honest picture of me inside his head so there can be no pretence. Does that sound strange? I guess I'm bossing my 'weird girl' era.

'I want to know who you are.' He points to the centre of my chest where my heart is beating, and I wonder if he can feel it as much as I can.

I take a moment to think. It makes me feel strange that I can't answer him immediately. I guess I've forgotten about dreams and aspirations. Since last summer, my main goal has been to get well. That's all. The dreams I had as a kid – whatever they were – seem to have moved aside to make way for other things, which sucks on many levels. I don't want everything to be about learning to navigate the heavy stuff. I want my dreams back. I want to find the things that make me tick again. That's the reason I came back to France in the first place. *Gaudium in veritate*.

'I want to . . . find my joy,' I say. I realise the answer is vague, but it's wholeheartedly the truth so I don't say anything else.

'Your joy?' he asks. 'Don't you have any of that?'

'Yeah, I do. I'm just . . . learning to get over something, and I feel like, by doing so, I've . . . overlooked the stuff that brings me joy.'

He nods slowly. 'I think it's smart of you to recognise that,' he says. 'Life can get heavy sometimes, and people forget how important it is to have fun. That's why I don't do social media – I prefer to be free, to live in the moment, you know? OK, so sticking with the theme . . . what's your most joyful memory?'

'Um . . . it'll be something to do with holidays,' I say. 'Like paddleboarding, or snorkelling in the Med, or eating rotisserie chicken in some French farmhouse exactly in the middle of nowhere. It's hard to pinpoint just one. You?'

'Same,' he says. 'I have so many great memories of Saint-Tropez, being on the beach at the bottom of my great-grandma's garden.'

His smile makes me smile too. 'We're going to Saint-Tropez this year,' I say. 'When will you be there?'

'We're going from here,' he says. 'I think we get there around the fifth.'

'We must be there at the same time,' I say, making a mental note to ask Pops. *I really hope we are*, I think.

'So aside from the "joy" search, what else makes you tick?' he asks.

I shrug. 'I like drawing. My dad is an art teacher, so I guess I get it from him. I like reading—'

'What's your favourite book?'

'The *dreaded* question! Um . . . I have no idea, but it will be something by Jennifer Niven.'

'*All the Bright Places*?' he asks.

'I knew you were going to say that,' I say. 'I love it, but I feel more connected to *Holding Up the Universe*.' *Because one of the main characters struggles with remembering*, I think. 'Actually, speaking of *All the Bright Places*, you give me serious "Finch" vibes.'

'Oh, really? So you see me as the charismatic love interest, eh?'

My cheeks flush because this isn't necessarily where I was going with this, although, yeah, I kinda do, but I can't admit that. I barely know him.

I push my trainers against the gravel so the swing starts moving because I'm sure he's flirting again, and it makes me feel strangely shy. He watches me swinging slowly, the creaking of the frame turning this moment into something comedically awkward and I can't help but smirk. When I catch his eye, he's smirking too.

'You can ask me something if you like,' he says.

'OK,' I say. 'Favourite colour?'

'You can do better than that, Iggy,' he says.

'Sorry,' I say. 'I didn't realise I was sitting next to the question police.'

'Technically you're *swinging* next to the question police.'

This makes me laugh out loud. 'I should've known,' I say. I begin to chew my bottom lip, the pressure to think of a great question strangely emptying my head for a moment. 'I've got one: if you could be reincarnated as any animal, what would it be?'

'Good question!' he says. 'Um . . . I don't know, how about a butterfly?'

'Cute, but why?'

'They only live for a couple of weeks, sometimes months, but sometimes only a day. I wouldn't put anything off. I'd live every day to the full like there's no tomorrow. That way I get to do it all.'

This makes me catch my breath. It's kinda beautiful.

'Most . . . embarrassing moment?' I ask, moving swiftly on before he notices me.

'Probably bumping into you with my paddleboard?'

'Stop!' I say, half laughing. 'That wasn't embarrassing *at all*. I'm actually really glad you did – otherwise we may never have met.'

'Oh, we would have,' he says. 'I would have made sure we bumped into each other some other way.'

He winks jokingly, and I feel it hit somewhere below my waistband. 'I'd forgotten you'd already seen me,' I say.

'Talking to the guy at the main house,' he says.

'Evan.'

'And he's a . . . friend?'

'I wouldn't exactly say that.'

'He's *more* than a friend?'

'What? No way! Absolutely not. I didn't mean that; he's a family friend, like our parents are friends and that's how we know each other. That's all.' The idea that Evan and I could be anything more makes me shudder.

We carry on volleying questions back and forth, and I think about how unlike me it is to meet someone like this on the first night of holidays. Evan's usually the one who has a whole group around him straightaway, whereas I'm a couple-of-days-in kind of gal. I'm glad I wasted no time with Roscoe. It actually feels like we're making a connection tonight, and as we learn more about one another, thanks to some top-tier banter and a hilarious round of quick-fire questions where we find out we both love pizza and the Disney film *Inside Out*, it blows my mind how contented I feel. I can't help but wonder what I would be doing now if our paddleboards hadn't collided. I'd probably be sitting somewhere on my own, avoiding Evan. Not very thrilling. But this? This couldn't be any more thrilling.

The park lights flicker on, bringing the night to life in a flurry of flying bugs. I tap my watch. It's later than I thought, even though it feels like we've only just started talking.

Not one part of me wants to leave him. The couple of hours we've spent together have been really fun, and there's still so much I want to know about him, and so much I want him to know about me too. But I've promised Pops and Dad I won't be late back, and breaking their trust now would be a bad move.

So we walk out of the park and through the trees, past the pizza restaurant and towards the tennis courts.

'What are you doing tomorrow?' he asks.

'I don't have any plans,' I reply.

'Would you like to do something . . . together?'

This isn't an answer I need to think about. I can think of nothing better than seeing him again. I want more of this; more of his special brand of humour, and charm, and flirting, and, yeah, *joy*.

'Yes,' I say.

'I'll meet you at the coach stop in the morning,' he says. 'Say, ten a.m.? I'll be counting down the seconds. G'night, Iggy.'

He stands to attention and does this phoney salute, before he heads away from me, turns back into the trees and then starts humming a tune to himself. He doesn't stick to the road, or any sort of path, he just weaves in and out of pine trees. Sticking to a path is what everybody else does.

But Roscoe couldn't be any less like everybody else.

SIX

There's already a group standing at the coach stop the next morning. I look for Roscoe among the excited faces that are already smothered in oily sun cream, but I don't see him. He isn't here yet, which gives me a heavy feeling in my stomach. I've already spent the last couple of hours worrying that he might not show, because I don't know him that well and he might be the type of person who does that. It's weird that I care so much, that someone who I barely know can seem so important, because, really, if he *doesn't* show it doesn't change anything. I'm still on holiday. I can still go back to the summer I was supposed to have, the summer with Pops and Dad, my family holiday and my crusade for joy. I could so easily slip back into that and never think of Roscoe again if I wanted to. Although even thinking about it makes the heavy feeling grow heavier. I really hope it doesn't come to that; I really hope he shows.

I take a seat on the wall by the coach stop and look across to the other side of the road. This is where I find him. Of course he's sitting over there, away from everybody else. I should have known.

'Hey,' I say, as I cross towards him.

'Morning,' he says, smiling.

The heavy feeling in my stomach instantly dissipates.

'Have you been sitting here long?'

'Not that long,' he says. Today his hair is loose and freshly washed, falling in glossy curls over his forehead, and his eyes look emerald green. 'What do you want to do today?'

'I don't mind,' I shrug. 'I haven't brought my board – I guess that's pretty obvious.'

The coach hisses around the corner and then rolls towards the waiting queue.

'We don't have to go to the beach, you know,' he says. 'We could go somewhere else, somewhere new – I just thought this would be a good place to meet.' He points to the side entrance of the campsite, where trees tower over the white-painted gates. 'That way looks interesting.'

My eyes thin as I look through the trees, trying to see what might lie beyond them. I already told Dad and Pops that I was going to the beach with friends. They know the beach; they know how regular the coach is, they know there are lifeguards, and so they let me go without question. I don't think they'd approve of me leaving the campsite with someone they don't know.

But then going on an adventure with Roscoe sounds way more exciting than going to the beach again, so I say, 'It *does* look interesting.'

We both wait, standing on the edge of the morning, wondering who will be brave enough to leap in first.

'Last one to the gate's a rotten egg,' Roscoe says, his face twisting into a mischievous smile.

'Oh, you're *so* going down,' I say.

Then I do it; we do it, we sprint side by side towards the gates of the campsite. I begin to laugh. It jumps around in my belly, shimmers in my bones, as I run as fast as I can.

'I win!' I shout, tapping my hand against the white-painted railing just before him. He bends over, his hands resting on his knees. I do a slow victory lap around him, holding my arms in the air.

'Hey – there's no need to rub it in!'

I lap him again for comedic effect. 'I'm a winner, baby!'

'You're quicker than I thought,' he says.

'That's me,' I say, holding my palm out flat by my hair so I look like the hand-tipping emoji. 'Always full of surprises.'

The French countryside offers up something different to what we have at home; something beautiful but abrasive at the same time, with rich dry earth, spiky green cacti and vibrant fruit trees, as well as row upon row of lush vineyards. I can almost taste its texture on my tongue, green and salty like capers.

'This is stunning,' I say, as we leave the forest that surrounds the campsite behind.

'The south of France is a special place,' he says, nodding in agreement.

His eyes glaze over, and I can only assume he's lost somewhere in a summer memory. I find myself wanting to go there too, wanting to follow him into his head so I can know more. I want to know what he was like as a kid, whether he went on the same sort of camper-van holidays as I did, what his family is like. I want to know everything, because knowing more means being closer to him, and even though we're walking side by side, I feel like it isn't quite close enough.

The road splits at what looks like a medieval tower. Beige, brown and white sandstone spirals up from the ground all the way to the top, where one side has crumbled away. Thick green vines burst through the ground and climb the tower, as if they would pull it back into the dirt. At the bottom there's a doorway. Roscoe walks up to it and I follow him, walking over a path that has been pushed apart by the roots of a nearby tree, and poke my head through the doorway. Inside there are more vines and frilly purple flowers. The tower has no roof, pale stones circling all the way to the sky, which is so blue it actually makes my eyes sting.

'This is beautiful,' I say, following Roscoe in. Pops would love this.

'Nice, isn't it?' he says. 'I prefer quieter places like this.'

I don't know any other guy who would prefer the ruins of a medieval tower to the beach, but for him this place makes sense. He, like this tower, stands alone in a landscape of fields. He's a rarity, one of a kind, which of course only makes him appeal to me even more.

'I forgot to ask where you're from?' I say, picking up where we left off last night.

'I'm Welsh,' he says, 'from Swansea.'

I knew there was an accent going on.

'My mum is French,' he continues, 'which is why we come to the Mediterranean every year. She likes me to see where she grew up. We do Italy most years too.'

'Oh, are you going to Italy this time?' I ask.

He nods. 'Portofino, Florence and Rome.'

'I'm going to Portofino!' I say excitedly. 'And Rome.'

I'd wondered if he would be on the same sort of holiday as me – a lot of people travel from campsite to campsite in Europe. I hope this means we're going to be in the same places at the same time. It would be amazing to spend an entire summer with him.

'Portofino is really nice,' he says. 'And Rome is . . .' He kisses his fingers in a chef's kiss. 'I love it.'

'I'm looking forward to it,' I say. 'I've never been.'

'You *have* to try this pizza place near Piazza Campo de Fiori. They do the crispiest pizza base ever . . .' He carries on, recommendations of places to visit and eat (mostly eat) pouring out of him, and I'm awestruck by his passion. I imagine us visiting Rome together. I see us eating gelato by the Trevi Fountain, touring the Coliseum, rowing on the lake in Villa Borghese, and all of the other places he suggests. My mind becomes a holiday mood board; postcards of famous landmarks and Instagram snaps of our smiling faces as we eat and laugh and . . . My eyes drop to his lips. How can I be feeling this way when I barely know him? In my head it makes no sense, but in my insides, in my guts and pumping heart, it feels so right.

'You know your Roman landmarks,' I say.

'Not really,' he says. 'That's the great thing about Rome – even though it's ancient, there's always something new to surprise you. Do you know when you'll be there?'

I shake my head. 'It's right at the end of the holiday, so, like, three or four weeks from now, I'm guessing.'

'I hope we're there at the same time. I'd like to show you around Rome, not just tell you about it.' He starts to bite his fingernail. 'Does that sound strange?'

'Maybe,' I say. 'But maybe I'm into strange.'
I love the way this makes him smile.

We come to a small village where the streets are close and twisting, with more of the flowers from the tower spilling over rooftops like purple waterfalls, and medieval archways burrowing beneath them. I stop at a bakery, because the smell is too good not to, and treat us to a warm, buttery croissant. The flaky pastry crumbles in my fingers as I tear it in half, and we sit by a fountain in the little square to eat it.

'Have you decided on your favourite holiday memory yet?' he asks.

'It's hard to choose just one,' I say.

I tilt my head up to the sky to think and, surprisingly, something appears. It's hazy at first, made up of echoes and shadows and blurred edges, but it keeps moving through the dark, pushing forwards as it sharpens . . .

I'm standing on the side of a pedalo. The sun is hot and high in a cloudless sky as I float on a reservoir; green water, hanging vines, willow branches and cliffs. I throw something into the water but my feet slip out from under me and I fall in. And all I can think is that I can't wait to get back to the surface so I can laugh. The laughter is sweet and intense and so stupidly joyful, and it's trapped inside, and I have to let it out. As soon as I break the surface it escapes me; I laugh harder than I think I've ever laughed before . . .

'One summer we took out a pedalo,' I say.

'Who did?' he asks.

'I'm . . . not sure,' I say. As much as I try to focus, the face of the person on the pedalo isn't clear.

'You don't know?' he asks.

I understand that it's weird for people to forget things like faces; faces are probably the first things we remember, and I should probably explain to him why I can't, but I don't want to take things to a dark place so soon. So I just shrug and say, 'Must've been my dad.'

As soon as I say it, I know it isn't true. I feel the lie turn sour in my mouth. There was somebody else next to me on the pedalo, somebody whose face is lost to me, only I'm too embarrassed to admit it.

'We laughed so hard when I fell in,' I say, trying to focus on the positive aspects of the memory.

It isn't hard to recall the feeling. It's still there, tucked safely inside me, murmuring beneath my ribcage like a second heartbeat. I look down at my lap, which is covered in croissant crumbs, because I think I'm about to laugh again – the memory is that strong – but it's too cringe to laugh for no reason.

'What?' he asks.

'Nothing,' I say, grinning to myself.

'What is it?'

'It was just . . . the way I fell in; the way I thought I was being so cool, throwing as hard as I could, and the force of it made me slip and fall . . . It was so . . . ridiculous . . .!' I burst into a fit of giggles that I can't stop. I laugh so hard every muscle in my body tenses up. It's as if I'm there again, reliving that perfectly joyful summer day. When I look up he's laughing too, tears at the corners of his eyes, and seeing him laugh only makes me laugh harder.

'Those dimples!' Roscoe beams.

'Stop,' I say, covering my face with my hands. 'I'm such an ugly laugher.'

'You're not at all,' he says, gripping my wrists and moving them away from my face. 'I think watching you laugh might have just shot to the top of my list of favourite things.'

His eyes meet mine and I feel a spark light somewhere in my belly. His eyes are extraordinary; mysterious and beautiful, but in an unexpected-beautiful sort of way. I keep finding things about his face that I like.

'Anyway,' I begin. 'Moving swiftly on – let's talk about you before I embarrass myself any further. What's your favourite holiday memory?'

'I think mine is the same as yours now,' he chuckles. 'I can picture you in my head, so elegant one minute and then hitting the water the next.'

I shove him playfully, and laugh so loud the sound bounces around the little square. I'm sure the locals think we're crazy, but I honestly don't care. I don't think I've laughed like this for a very long time. Maybe since the pedalo memory.

I'd forgotten how good it can make you feel.

Music starts playing in the square, drifting through an open window. It isn't music I've heard before; it sounds old and crackling, thick and distorted. Still, it's pretty music, the introduction played by strings and wood instruments before a French singer begins.

Roscoe smiles and tilts his head to the side. 'This song is

called "La Vie en Rose",' he says. 'It reminds me of my great-grandma's house in Saint-Tropez.' He begins to sway, closing his eyes as he falls into another summer memory. 'It's like taking a deep breath, isn't it? How music can invoke a memory. *Hmm hmm hmm hmm hmm hmm.* I can see my grandparents dancing on the balcony at the back of the house. *Ya da da da da da da.* The sun setting over the sea behind them. *La la la la la la.*' He pushes himself up and offers me his hand. 'Will you dance with me, Iggy?'

'What – here?' I ask.

He wiggles his fingers. 'Don't be shy. There's nobody around.'

Nobody has asked me to dance with them before. I'm not even sure how to dance, and I really don't want to make a fool of myself in front of him, but I really want to try, really want to hold his warm body close to mine. 'Don't laugh if I fall,' I say, taking his hand. 'I feel like I've done enough of that in front of you already.'

'Would falling be so bad?' he asks, pulling me closer.

I think I'm beginning to understand the true meaning of falling for someone. It isn't gentle or subtle; it's sudden, it's abrupt. Like falling off a cliff; it happens all at once.

How can I feel this way for someone I've only known for a day?

He begins to sway me, and turn me, and dip me, and I find myself laughing again. This laughter is different – it isn't the hard, hysterical laughter of the pedalo memory, but something softer, warming my insides, like the first gulp of delicious hot chocolate. I have to close my eyes because I think I'm being awkward as hell.

'What are you thinking?' he asks.

'That I'm . . . a terrible dancer,' I say.

'No, you're not,' he says. 'I know you can feel the music – I can tell by the way you're moving your body.'

I feel my shoulders move a little closer to my ears. Nobody has ever talked about my body like this before. In truth, I'm self-conscious. I know it isn't perfect.

'You look radiant,' he whispers, twirling me under his arm. I feel light, like I could spin into the sky.

The song finishes but we keep swaying. I open my eyes, meeting his, and I have to look away because I don't want him to see what I'm thinking. It's too soon to be thinking this way. Isn't it?

'I love that song,' he says. 'You'll think of me when you hear it now.'

'I totally will,' I say jovially. Although something tells me I won't need a song to remember him by. 'When can I see you again?' It's out of character for me to be so forward, but I already want another day of this. Of his smile, his laughter, his way of making everything seem brighter. He is exactly the kind of summer I've been looking for.

'I'm standing right here,' he chuckles.

'I know,' I say, 'but we need to keep exploring the campsite.' It's a thinly veiled excuse to see him again, and if I wasn't feeling so dreamlike maybe I could have come up with something better, but I am, and so I throw him an enthusiastic smile in the hope he feels the same.

'I guess we do,' he shrugs. 'But I think it's way more exciting out here.'

He spreads his arms wide and spins around.

He's right, I think. Out here we can laugh and dance as freely as we like, and not have to answer to anybody, only each other.

SEVEN

I don't know what I expected this summer to be, but if this is how it's starting I can't wait to see what unfolds. Being with Roscoe is like a dream. Granted, after last summer the bar was set pretty low, but Roscoe coming into my life feels so unexpectedly brilliant that I can't help wondering what the rest of summer has in store for me.

'How did you sleep, Iggs?' asks Dad as I emerge from the camper-van a few mornings after we danced to 'La Vie en Rose' in the square.

'Fine,' I say, joining him and Pops at the breakfast table.

'All ready for Marseille?' asks Pops excitedly.

Today we're going on a city excursion. Pops loves a city excursion. He'll have a full itinerary planned for the day, no doubt.

'Um, yeah,' I say. 'I'm looking forward to it.'

This isn't strictly true. Now Roscoe is on the scene, I'm not really interested in doing anything other than spending time with him. Even the prospect of Marseille can't excite me that much. All I can think about is getting back so I can see him again.

'How was the beach yesterday?' asks Dad. 'Evan said he went too. You could have caught the coach together.' He points over the road to the Redwoods' breakfast table.

'Put your arm down,' I hiss.

'Why?' he whispers back.

'Oh, morning, Iggy,' shouts Evan.

'Morning,' I say, as nicely as I can.

I don't want to be mean to him, I'm *so* not about that, but at the same time he's grating on me in ways I didn't expect this year. I know I've always found him annoying, but where before his general lack of respect drove me to distraction, this year there are other things bothering me.

Firstly, this good-guy persona. Like, why am I the only one who remembers what he was like before? Pops thinks he's the best thing since cinnamon sugar, and he already has a big group of friends on the campsite who probably think the same, which is baffling to me because, deep inside, he's still the same person he's always been.

Secondly, and this may be even more surprising, he's been pretty overbearing this year. Before, he would laugh at me as soon as our parents weren't around, but now he greets me first thing with a friendly '*Morning, Iggy*', or in the evening with a jovial '*How was your day?*'. I mean, it's nice but it feels fake and forced and it's starting to bug me. Like, did I imagine the person he was before? Was that all in my head? I could just about cope with the old Evan from a very comfortable distance, but this new guy won't give me the space to do that, and my parents forcing him on me is starting to make me feel claustrophobic.

'I don't need Evan to go anywhere with me,' I whisper. 'I'm fine on my own.'

Pops looks up from his iPad and stares at me for longer than is comfortable, which makes me look away. I know he thinks I'm being childish, but it isn't going to change anything. Evan and I are incompatible as friends. That's all there is to it.

I take a bite out of one of the pastries that are sitting in the middle of the table and all at once the taste of vanilla custard hits my tongue.

'Crème pâtissière,' says Dad as I moan with delight. 'Delicious, aren't they?'

'Divine,' I say, reaching for another and dumping it on my plate.

'There's plenty more,' says Pops. 'Are you bringing a bag today, Iggy?'

'Yeah, I'll bring my yellow bag,' I say. 'I'd like to pick something up in a gift shop.'

'I'll pack some snacks,' says Pops. 'There are always plenty of gaps in the schedule for snack breaks.'

Marseille is unexpectedly pretty. A basilica looms above the old port atop a mountain, a golden statue of the Virgin Mary glimmering in the morning sunlight at its highest point, like a candle on a cake. It should come as a surprise that I could forget visiting a place as beautiful as this last year, but I'm more used to forgetting than remembering these days. I suppose this gives me the chance to rediscover places like Marseille, seeing them as if for the first time with fresh eyes.

We have lunch in a seafood restaurant with excellent views across the harbour, mopping up mussels in a tomato, garlic and chilli bisque with crusty French bread. It gets a little messy, and the white tablecloth and napkins are soon smeared with splotches of red sauce, but the mussels are so good. It doesn't matter how understated a restaurant looks from the outside, the food in France is always delicious. This is something I do remember.

After a visit to a neo-Byzantine cathedral, it's on to the gift shops.

This is the part I've been looking forward to most. Collecting objects has become important to me because they hold the key to memories. It's crazy how something inanimate, like a shell, can unlock a part of my brain. Only last week I found a wooden bottle opener I'd forgotten about in my holiday bag, and I was transported back to a flea market in the Loire Valley. It's as if I'm collecting puzzle pieces and the more I find, the surer of myself I become.

The first shop we visit has dreamcatchers by the door, which draws me in straight away. I love dreamcatchers; the idea that something physical could capture something as whimsical as dreams is everything to me. I have two or three at home already. The long beads and feathers sway in the breeze as I walk into the shop, looking for something that screams 'Marseille', but in an understated way. I want to give Roscoe a gift when I see him. I want him to know that I've missed hanging out with him, and a gift feels like a cute way of doing that.

As I'm browsing at the back of the store, where the shelves are filled with leather bracelets and statues of the Virgin Mary, I see that people have written on the edges of the shelves. Names, initials, social media handles, hearts and scribbles cover the exposed wood; some of the writing dates back as far as 2014. I run my hand along 'D+T' and 'Molly Frost, Dallas

Texas' and a heart with 'Jose and Ally' written inside. I wonder who started this tradition. It's almost like an exchange; buying a souvenir to take a piece of the city with you, but leaving a trace of yourself behind too.

'Did you find anything?' asks Pops, appearing from behind a stack of moving postcards.

'I think I'm going to take this,' I say, taking a leather bracelet from the shelf.

It's black leather, with three smaller pieces that weave together to make the strap, and 'Marseille' stitched into a solid piece on top. I think Roscoe will like it.

I show it to Pops and his face changes, quickly moving from bright and sunny to shadowed, as if a cloud has just come over it. He takes the bracelet from me, turning it around in his hands, and then looks from it to me.

'Why do you want this bracelet?' he asks.

'What do you mean?' I ask.

'This bracelet . . .' he begins. 'It's . . . why does it have to be *this* one?'

'It doesn't *have* to be this one,' I say. 'I just think . . . it's nice.'

He looks at it as if it means something to him, like this bracelet is more than a cute reminder of Marseille but something else. Maybe even something dark.

'What's wrong?' I ask.

He twists it around in his hand, studying it, before passing it back to me.

'Nothing,' he says, smiling. 'If that's the one you like, then get it.'

'Why are you being weird?' I ask, not taking the bracelet from him.

'I'm not,' he says.

'You know you are. You just looked at that bracelet like Gollum looks at the ring.'

'That's a tad dramatic, Iggy,' he says. 'Do they do it in other colours?'

He shakes it in mid-air and I take it from him. 'They have it in brown and white,' I say. *But black will suit Roscoe better*, I think.

'How nice,' he says, looking at the shelf.

I follow him because that reaction was way too suspicious. It's so unlike Pops to be this way. I don't believe he's done a single suspicious thing in his life.

As I watch him scan the shelf, his face unmoving, I notice something. There, among the jumble of so many other names of people from all over the world, I see two I recognise:

Iggy & Roscoe

I stare at the letters drawn in black Sharpie, how they curl and flick in ways I recognise not only because the names are familiar, but the handwriting too. I reach forward and brush my hand against it.

'Some people probably think this looks messy,' says Pops, reappearing behind me. 'But I actually think it's quite marvellous – like these shelves are a piece of art and can tell a story of their own.'

He's so right. These shelves *are* telling a story, they're trying to tell *me* a story, I think, but it isn't making sense yet. I'm not following the plot. Did I just write these names? I can think of no other reason why they'd be here. But I don't see how that's possible. Did I just write them and forget? I feel so confused right now, which is a feeling I've become familiar with this past year, and it frightens me. I begin to feel hot, the air in the shop too thick to inhale properly, and I think I'm about to panic.

I quickly pay for the bracelet, dropping the coins as I pass them to the cashier and almost knocking over a display of postcards in my rush to leave the shop.

'Did you see it?' asks a voice.

I don't even need to look up. I would recognise his voice anywhere now.

'What are you doing here?' I ask. I had no idea he was visiting Marseille today too.

'Surprise!' he says, standing by the doorway looking very pleased with himself.

I want to hug him, want to reach out and take his hands in mine and pull him closer to me, because I know this would stop the onset of panic.

'Did you see the shelf?' he asks.

'You did that?' I ask.

The clouds in my head begin to thin into mist so I'm able to see through them again. *Roscoe was the one who wrote our names on the shelf*, I think. It wasn't my handwriting. It wasn't me, there's no need to feel scared; he wanted to leave a part of us here, wanted to add our names to the other holidaymakers'.

'This way you can't forget,' he says. 'We're here for always.'

Always, I think, and my stomach tightens into clasped hands.

'That's really lovely,' I say.

'*Ig-gy*,' I hear Dad call from the street outside. I look over Roscoe's shoulder to see him waving me over.

'I was wondering,' I say. 'Can I see you tomorrow?'

I want more of him. I want more of the person I'm becoming when I'm around him. He's just proven himself to be the antidote I've needed all along, because now I don't feel panicked and confused, only happy to see him. I don't want to take my chances with this feeling; it seems too important.

'Want to explore?' he says with a glint in his eye. 'Meet me at the coach stop again.'

'What are you doing over there?' Pops calls.

'I should probably go,' I say. 'I'm here with my parents.' I take a step back, but I don't turn away from him yet. I have one final thing I want him to know, which now feels so much more important than it did when I walked in. 'I'm happy when I'm with you, Roscoe,' I say.

Then I leave the gift shop, dreamcatchers swirling around me like magic.

EIGHT

The next morning, Dad and Pops head to the pool.

After they leave, I throw my towel and sun cream into my bag and lock the camper-van up. But I've barely cleared our pitch when a voice calls me back.

'Hey, Iggy,' they say. 'Wait up!'

I turn to see Evan Redwood hurrying along the road behind me, his hair poking out from underneath a baseball cap and a beach towel thrown around his shoulders.

'You heading to the pool?' he asks.

I shake my head.

'The beach?'

I nod.

'Do you mind if I walk with you?'

'Sure.'

'I'm meeting some of the guys,' he says. 'Are you meeting anybody?'

I shake my head. I'm trying to keep verbal contact to a minimum because he always used to laugh at my voice, repeating what I said, making me sound breathy and stupid. When a person treats you this way, you never forget it.

'There's a really big group of us this year,' he continues. 'We hang out at the pool most days – some of them are coming to the same campsites in Italy too . . .'

I don't acknowledge him. I just keep walking as if he isn't by my side. Does this make me a bad person? Should I just let it go? I don't think I want to. This holiday isn't about forgetting, it's about remembering, and he can't just switch on me like this. It's too much: the image change, the friendly approach, the walking me to the coach stop as if he's my new holiday bestie, it's beyond unsettling and I'm not about that energy.

'. . . then there's Lucy and Jade,' he continues. 'They're from Manchester. I think you'd get on with them, they're funny, like you—'

'What are you doing?' I ask, stopping suddenly.

'Sorry?' he asks.

'Like, right now,' I say. 'What are you trying to do?'

'I'm not trying to do anything,' he says.

'You . . . *don't like me*, Evan. You've never liked me. You've been awful to me ever since we met, and now you're being overly nice, and it's just . . . *too much* . . . It's too much, and I want to know why.'

Our families may be close, but we're not, and we never have been. It's ridiculous to think that we could be, as if we can wipe away all those years of clashing. Is this because his mum has told him to play nice this year? I want him to see that he doesn't need to be this way. I'm not fragile. I'm fine. Actually, I'm better than fine and I don't need him to make any sort of fuss.

He turns round to face me and I look at him properly, maybe for the first time in the five summers I've known him. He looks sad, wounded even, like somehow we've switched roles.

How am I now suddenly able to hurt Evan Redwood so easily, when before he didn't care about a single thing I said?

'Look, I'm *so* here for people embracing their truth,' I begin, 'and, yeah, you're way nicer this year, which is great, but . . . I just can't forget everything that's happened.'

I don't think I can put it clearer than that, and I'm expecting him to take this on the chin and walk away, but I can see from the look in his eyes, see from the many questions that seem to be appearing behind them, that he isn't. This admission, though it seems clear to me, has only made him even more confused.

'You . . . remember then?' he asks.

'Of course I remember,' I say. 'Last summer might be a bit iffy, but all of the ones before it, all of the teasing and laughing – well, that stuff sticks.'

'So you *don't* remember?' he asks.

'Am I not being clear?' I say. 'I just said—'

'*I meant last summer,*' he says darkly. 'You don't remember *any* of it?'

I take a frustrated breath and sigh a frustrated sigh, because *he* of all people must know the answer. 'Evan, I'm going to say this now and I really want you to listen to me,' I begin. 'This might sound harsh, but I would appreciate it if you would leave me alone this year.'

He doesn't acknowledge me, just keeps staring.

'Evan, did you—'

'You know it wasn't my fault, right?' he says, taking a step towards me. 'I tried to make it right. I *really* tried.'

'What are you talking about?'

'I did everything I could . . . I tried. I really did . . .'

'What do you mean – tried what?'

'It wasn't my fault!'

His words ring like an echo as pain stabs into the side of my head. I press my hands against my temples, closing my eyes so everything goes black, no trees or tents or tennis courts, only black.

And then I hear it.

Laughter.

High-pitched, pointed laughter, sharp enough to move my insides, stabs into my head.

'Iggy?' says a distant voice. 'Iggy, what's wrong?'

'Nothing,' I hear myself say. *Nothing is wrong with me.*

'You've gone pale,' he says. 'Here, do you want some water?'

'I don't need water,' I say, raising my hands.

Water, I think. *I'm underwater. I'm thrashing below the surface like a rag doll, wrapped in a confusing cocoon of bubbles and foam. I know the best way to survive this is to float; there's no point trying to fight water, I have to go with it, but first I need to find the surface. I try to kick my legs, but they won't budge, as if they're no longer mine. They quiver beneath me, my feet contracting in strange ways. My insides begin to press together as I panic, my lungs pulling downwards. I'm going down instead of up, away from the light, moving to colder waters. My chest begins to convulse as it spasms. I'm sinking, trapped in some horrible nightmare that I'll never escape.*

'Iggy?' he says.

I open my eyes and I'm back in sunshine and warm, abundant air, solid ground beneath my feet. Evan Redwood is standing over me, a look of concern on his face.

'What . . . happened?' I ask.

'Here.' He passes me the bottle of water. 'Take a sip.'

This water does as it's supposed to; it eases my panic and soothes me from the inside out. I take in the deepest, slowest breath I can and count to four, like Sian Steadman told me to, my shoulders raising all the way to my ears. It isn't easy. I'm shaking.

'Don't tell my parents,' I say. It's the first thing I can think of to say; how Pops and Dad would worry if they knew about this episode.

'I won't,' he says.

'Promise me, Evan,' I say.

'I promise.'

I push myself back, using the tree to help me stand.

'Take it easy,' Evan says.

'I'm OK,' I lie. 'I just want to go to the coach stop.'

My legs are unsteady, but I have to walk, I have to keep putting one foot in front of the other, just like I did in the hospital.

'Shouldn't you go back to your camper-van? Have a lie down?'

I ignore him. 'All right. Then I'll come with you,' he says.

'I'm fine on my own,' I say.

'Please, let me help you,' he says, placing his hand under my elbow.

'No!' I say, snatching it back. 'Really, Evan – I don't need you to help me. Just go to the pool with your friends and . . . leave me alone.'

NINE

This time Roscoe and I do take the coach because I want to be as far away from the campsite as possible. But when everybody else piles on to the beach, with towels, umbrellas and inflatables wedged under their arms, we walk in the opposite direction to see what else we might find.

Ten minutes away from the coach stop, we stumble across a market set out along a road that leads to a church. There are a couple of hot-food vans parked up at this end, and so I get us a cup of fresh doughnuts, laced with sugar, and we eat them as we explore the stalls.

'Pops would love this,' I say, picking up a bowl with a quirky fruit pattern around the rim. Pops has a passion for pottery, and the weirder the better.

This market has the standard fruit and veg stalls, clothing stalls and stalls stacked high with kitchen accessories like washing-up bowls and mop buckets, but it's also more traditional, with sprigs of French lavender for sale, handmade leather bags swinging above our heads and even an old-fashioned wooden caravan painted bright red. As we walk down the main street, keeping to the shaded side as it gets hotter by the minute, I notice a person sitting on the steps outside the caravan with wavy bleached hair that frames their forehead in a halo of fuzz, and a facial tattoo of a bird on their cheek.

'Let me tell your fortune,' they say, their dark eyes meeting mine. They have a thick French accent, but know to speak to us in English.

'I'm OK,' I say, holding up my hand.

'There are two people in your life,' they say, ignoring my rejection. 'One with your best interests at heart, one with your worst. Come – let me tell you about them.'

They hold out their hand as if they want me to go into the caravan, and I shake my head again. I notice there's a chalkboard next to their feet which has 'Thirty euros' written on it.

'Really, I'm OK,' I say. 'Thank you.'

I've never been into things like fortune telling. I'm not here for some generic spiel, like how eight will be a lucky number for me, or how something exciting will happen on Thursday, which is crazy steep. I'm not sure I believe a person can tell you your fortune, or future or whatever.

'Wait!' they shout as we turn to leave. 'Quand les arbres se balancent et que la rivière coule à rebours.'

People turn and look at me, and I want the ground to swallow me up, so I grab Roscoe by the wrist and pull him off the main road.

'What was that?' I whisper. He understands French far better than I do.

'Something about rivers flowing backwards,' he says.

'For real?' I ask, my stomach sinking. *Why would they mention rivers?*

'That's what it sounded like,' he says.

I pull Roscoe further along the road, keen to distance myself from the fortune teller. I don't want to think about rivers, not here, not today.

The town is artsy and vibrant, and even the church at the end of the road looks unlike any other I've seen. It's so far from traditional that it sort of redefines what a church could be; it looks more like a piece of art. It shoots out of the ground in columns like stalagmites, as if it's been built by nature, not people. This place has Pops written all over it. I wonder if he knows about it, or if we came here last year?

When the doughnuts are done, we head back along the promenade to the far side of the beach where the coastline juts out in a cliff. We climb stone steps and follow a path as it meanders alongside the sea until we come to a picnic bench.

'It's hot,' I say, removing my water bottle from my rucksack and taking a swig. The cold water hits my belly, spreading icy roots across my hot insides. 'And that's so cold,' I say, gasping.

The sun shines a diamond pathway across the sea, and I feel a kernel of excitement inside. The vastness of the Mediterranean always gives me a thrill, and I don't think that will ever change. It's so huge and powerful that I'm reminded of how small I am, how susceptible I am to the elements in this place with hard cliff edges and vast seas and searing heat. The Iggy from back home, whose world had become so small, feels like a distant memory here. I'm curious again. I have an appetite again, as big as the sea, and I think I have the person sitting next to me to thank for this.

'Can you deal with that view?' I ask.

'I know – stunning,' he says. 'This is why it's always better to explore; you get to find all the magical places.'

'Magical is the word,' I say.

'Magical *is* the word,' he says. 'Hey, did I tell you about the magician?'

'Oh no, this sounds like the start of a joke . . .' I say.

'We had to stop hanging out in the end . . . he kept disappearing.'

Without meaning to, I spit out my water. 'That is baaaad!' I say.

'Hey – why are good magician's assistants so hard to find?'

'Are we seriously doing this?'

'Because they're highly sawed after.'

His laughter is infectious; the more he laughs, the more I do too. In a flash we're both doubled over, red-faced, laughing at each other laughing.

'Those jokes are ter-ri-ble,' I say, separating the word for emphasis.

'OK – last one,' he says. 'What kind of dog does magic tricks?'

'I don't know – what kind of dog does magic tricks?'

'A labracadabrador!'

'That's so . . . stupid!' I say, laughter stuttering through my throat.

I glance sideways at him, and I feel my belly fill up with so many wings that I could take off across the water, following the path laid out by the sun. He's so warm and bright and funny, but earthy at the same time, with gravel in his voice and heat in his hands. He's wild and exciting and makes me feel things I thought I'd lost, and no matter how close I am to him right now it simply isn't close enough. I want to be closer.

'I'm a collector of dad jokes,' he says. 'I have a dad joke for all occasions.'

'Weddings, birthdays, bat mitzvahs . . .' I say.

'Exactly! You never know when you might have to whack out a dad joke. You'd be surprised how effective they are in icebreaker situations.'

'This is like social survival 101,' I say.

'Stick with me, kid,' he says in a phoney American gangster accent. 'We'll laugh our way through anything.'

I take another swig of cold water and notice there's a red admiral butterfly sunbathing on the stone walkway in front of us. Its wings are orange and black, and dotted with white. The colours look vivid in the sunlight, like I'm looking at them in high definition. I lean closer to it, and as if it knows it takes off again, flapping right in front of my face, before resting on my knee.

'Whoa!' I say, sitting taller. 'I've never had one land on me before.'

I hold my breath, the butterfly delicately balancing on my skin, its legs as fine as the tiny white hairs growing there. I'm reminded of the park and what Roscoe said about being a butterfly.

'Do they really not live long?' I ask.

'Some of them,' he shrugs.

I watch its petal-like wings; its fragility, its beauty, and I remember something Pops once said to me. 'After my grandma died, Pops told me that butterflies represent the people we've lost,' I say. 'I guess that's Pops all over – he's always searching for the rainbow.'

'That's nice.' Roscoe smiles. Gently, he brushes his thumb against my bottom lip to wipe away a dusting of doughnut sugar. 'This is nice too,' he says.

The butterfly flits away again, this time towards the sea and away from us, but the wings in my stomach are beating stronger than ever.

'Yeah,' I say. 'It so is.'

TEN

That night I meet Roscoe just outside the campsite. I wait until Pops and Dad are deep in their poker game with the Redwoods, before I climb out of the camper-van window and make my way along the back road to the main entrance, checking over my shoulder to make sure I'm not being followed.

I hurry along the road in darkness, taking a sharp left when I come to the end of the campsite until I'm facing the peach orchard. The trees have long, twisted arms that are full with fruit, the fresh green smell of unripe peaches filling my nose as I hurry over uneven ground, away from the road.

I find Roscoe in an opening, lit by starlight, sitting cross-legged at the foot of a peach tree. As soon as he sees me he jumps to his feet.

'Hey!' he says. 'I was starting to worry.'

'Sorry,' I say. 'I had to wait until my parents were occupied.'

'Come take a seat next to me,' he says. 'The sky is so clear tonight. Breathtaking, actually – it looks faultless from down here.'

I sit beside him and see that there's an opening in the branches above our heads. It takes a moment for my eyes to focus properly, stars appearing one by one until the sky is as big as anything I've ever seen. There must be thousands of stars, thrown across the black in wild shapes, twisting around one another in a kaleidoscopic arrangement that leaves my eyes crossing.

'That's Ursa Major,' says Roscoe. 'Do you see the body and head? It's supposed to look like a big bear. There's Ursa Minor too.'

'I'm guessing that's a little bear,' I say.

He smiles at me, and it's even brighter than the stars. 'Don't you think they're amazing?' he asks. 'Like, how do they exist? How did they start?'

'I've never thought about it before,' I say.

'They're literally floating balls of plasma, which sounds so ordinary, but they're utterly special.' I see the stars alive in his eyes as he tilts his face upwards. 'There's Draco and Lyra,' he says, sketching a line across the sky with his finger, 'and Hercules. The stars are constant. They don't change. There's something reassuring about that, don't you think?'

It's as if there's an invisible bond between us, drawing me to him. I didn't know people could be this way; I didn't think the stuff people are made of could be magnetic. But he is, we are, and it's the strangest, most brilliant thing.

'You know so much,' I say. 'Which year are you in at school, by the way?' It seems strange that I don't know this already.

'Thirteen,' he answers.

'I'm just about to go into Year Twelve. At a different school, though.'

'Are you nervous?'

I shrug. 'I think I'm ready for a change. Year Eleven was a bit of a wipe-out.'

'How come?'

My mind carries the conversation on, playing out different possible outcomes of what would happen if tonight was the night I opened up to Roscoe about last summer. I go quiet as I follow the threads. I don't want him to think of me as being damaged or fragile or any of the other things people have thought about me this past year. I want a fresh start with him. I want to be the Iggy I was before, and I feel so close to that person when I'm with him. But I don't want there to be secrets between us either. This is my truth era. *Gaudium in veritate.* So I say, 'I was in a pretty bad accident last year. I fell in a river and nearly died.'

'I'm so sorry,' he says.

'I'm fine,' I say. 'It's just there have been a lot of adjustments this year. I actually missed the first month of Year Eleven, and I've been in therapy since the accident, so I've felt a little removed from the person I was before.'

'That sounds tough,' he says. 'How are you feeling now?'

'I don't know,' I begin, treading carefully because talking about this can trigger anxious feelings and that's the last thing I want. 'There are things I don't remember. About last summer, I mean.'

'Do you remember anything about the accident?' he asks.

I automatically go to the place in my head where that particular memory is kept. But, like always, all I find is darkness. 'Nothing at all,' I say. 'It's like it never happened.' Sometimes I wonder if it actually did, or if I'm making the whole thing up. Sometimes my feet feel rooted in the here and now, but my head feels like it's somewhere else entirely. 'I'm hoping that by going back to the place it happened, to Dijon, I find answers,' I continue.

'What do your parents say about that?' he asks.

'They don't say much. I mean – they're amazing. I couldn't ask for more support. They didn't leave my bedside when I was in hospital, and I can talk to them about anything. It's just, sometimes I think it's best to keep things to myself. Both of my parents work so hard, they don't need to hear about my struggles.'

'I think you're brave to come back here,' he says. 'You need to give yourself more credit – a lot of people would have run in fear.'

'I needed to come back,' I say. '*Gaudium in veritate.*'

'What does that mean?'

'It's Latin – it means "joy in truth". It basically means I have to find out what happened last summer, and then I'll be able to find my joy again.'

He goes quiet, and I feel myself holding my breath, because his silence could mean, well, anything.

'But what if you don't?' he asks eventually. 'Like – what if you go searching for something, and end up finding something you wish you hadn't, and it makes you feel worse?'

'It won't,' I say.

'You don't know that.'

'Whatever happened, I need to know.'

'But why?' he asks. 'I know you said you don't like to feel out of control, but do you really need to know everything to feel joyful again? You can feel joyful right now, starting today, right here with me, if you want.'

He places his hand on my knee, and when he touches me my skin feels tingly and warm. 'Do you think,' I begin, 'we could catch up again in Saint-Tropez?'

He smiles. 'I'd really like that.'

I don't want him to be just *somebody*, like the holiday friends from summers past who I made empty promises to keep in touch with. I haven't known him for long, but time moves differently on holiday. This connection we've made feels stronger than anything I've felt before. I can feel it by just being near him, as if it's something tangible, as if I could grip it with my hands like a shell from the seabed or a peach from a tree.

'And then Portofino?' I say. 'And Rome?'

'I could think of nothing better than spending more time with you,' he says.

My heart swells, sending warmth through my chest and down my arms. 'Oh, before I forget – I have something for you.' I reach into my pocket and take out the bracelet. 'I got this in the gift shop in Marseille. Here – try it on.'

He holds out his wrist as I fasten it for him, and then he sticks his thumb and little finger out and tilts his hand backwards and forwards to show it off. 'I love it,' he says. 'Thank you.'

He picks up my hand and, pressing our palms together, slides his fingers through the gaps. 'I'm really glad I met you, Iggy.'

We're looking at each other now, and I've never been this close to someone, close enough to feel their gentle breath as it brushes against the raised hairs on my arms, and close enough to feel their heat. I wonder if we could get closer still, and what that would be like, and how sweetly my heart would sing if we did.

'I'm glad I met you too,' I whisper.

ELEVEN

On Saturday, Dad and Pops get up early to visit the nearby food market. I don't even hear them leave, so I'm still in bed when they return laden with shopping bags filled with some of the biggest fruit and vegetables I've ever seen. Seriously, I didn't know tomatoes could grow bigger than your hand.

'Oh, you're here,' says Pops, removing his sunhat. 'I thought you would be at the beach.'

'What time is it?' I mumble.

'It's gone twelve,' he says.

Roscoe and I talked well into the night, and I didn't get back until the early hours of this morning, somehow managing to sneak into the camper-van without my parents noticing. I stretch my arms above my head as I think about how we opened up to each other about things I've never talked about with anybody else.

'What's with the smile?' Pops asks

I usually tell Dad and Pops everything. We have an open dialogue between us, and I don't want to lie to him, but I want to keep Roscoe to myself. I'm sure there'll come a day when I introduce him to my parents and they'll want to invite him round for dinner and interrogate him about his favourite food, his favourite art, his favourite everything, but, for now at least, I like that it's just us . . . and the stars.

'I'm not smiling,' I say, which makes me smile even more.

'Okaaay,' says Pops.

'Oh, is Iggs here?' asks Dad, poking his head into the camper-van. 'I thought you'd be out. We never see you any more.'

'Can you believe the size of these oranges?' asks Pops, holding one up that's roughly the size of a cantaloupe. 'The market was so divine – you would have loved it, Iggy. There was an entire building for seafood, and then another for meat and poultry. Oh, there was a doughnut van there too. I would have brought you some back, but I think they're best enjoyed fresh. They have a mid-week market so we can go again before we leave, if you like?' He waits for some sort of response, but I'm lost in a daydream about Roscoe's thumb brushing doughnut sugar from my lip. 'What is going on with you?' Pops asks. 'Are you sure you're OK? You look a little . . .'

'I'm just having a lazy morning,' I say. 'That's allowed, isn't it?'

'Of course it's allowed,' says Pops. 'That's what holidays are for. I don't think you should spend all day in here though, my love. Not when the world is so beautiful.' He continues unpacking, and I collapse back into my squishy pillow. 'I'm going to make a quick tomato salad – just a Nigella recipe – and then we can all head to the pool after lunch, if you like?'

'Sounds good to me,' says Dad.

They both look at me expectantly, and a guilty feeling spreads through my insides. They've gone to so much effort to make this holiday special for me. Yet somehow it's been over a week already and I've been MIA for most of it.

'Me too,' I say, giving them my widest smile.

The tomatoes taste unlike anything I've ever tasted before. Every mouthful is like sunshine. Pops mixes them with chopped onions and olives, and drizzles them with his own dressing made with fresh lemons, oil, salt and pepper.

Afterwards we head to the pool. It's very busy when we arrive. I imagine people get here early to grab the best spots, and we've left it a little late in the day. Still, we manage to find three sunbeds on the far side by the bar, sitting under the shade of an olive tree.

'How gorgeous is this?' asks Dad, dumping his bag on to one of the beds.

All of my family love the water, and no sooner have we laid our towels out than we're diving in. The pool is unheated and it shocks me awake, any tiredness I'd felt from the night before stripped away in a flash. I swim all the way to the other end and back again, only coming up for air three times, and it strikes me that this might be the first time I've swum properly since last summer. It's crazy to think that it's been a whole year since I've done this; stretched and glided through the water like it's the easiest thing in the world. There's something about being held in water; you have to give yourself over to it to learn how it moves so you can manoeuvre around it. I slip back into it easily, like riding a bike or a paddleboard, which makes me really happy. It would have been awful if last year had ruined this for me too.

After my last length, I scoop myself on to the side and watch Dad and Pops swimming together in the shallows, looking happier than I've seen either of them in a long time, and I feel their happiness in my chest. This makes me think about something Roscoe said last night, about searching for my joy. He said I could feel joyful right now, starting today, and I wonder if he might be right.

'Hey.'

I turn to see Evan Redwood sitting beside me. I didn't even notice he was there.

'Hi,' I say.

I haven't seen him since the episode yesterday morning, which means I feel more than a little awkward. I feel bad for snapping at him. I actually think it was good of him to stay to make sure I was OK. The old Evan never would have done that, and this has to mean he has changed for the better.

'It's a decent pool, isn't it?' he says.

'Yeah, it's nice,' I say.

I press my lips together, rubbing them back and forwards as I try to pluck up the courage to say what I want to say to him.

'Listen, I—' I begin.

'Iggy, I'm—' he says at exactly the same time. 'Sorry. You first.'

'I just wanted to say ... thanks for yesterday,' I say. 'I'm grateful that you were there and that you looked after me.'

'Any friend would have done the same,' he says.

Friend. Is it possible we really could be friends? I know it would be easier than arguing all the time.

'I'm sorry if I've been stand-offish,' I say. 'I was expecting you to be the same guy from last year, and I see now that you're not. I actually think it's really great that you've made such positive changes.'

'I had to change,' he says surely. 'You know I did.'

I shrug. 'I'm not really sure what I know any more,' I say. 'But I *do* know that holding a grudge is silly, and so I'd like it if we could . . . start over?'

He smiles, and I think it might be the first time I've seen him smile properly since we got here. 'Does this mean you'll be joining in with our poker games?' he asks. 'Your dad is killing it, by the way – he's won nearly every game.'

'He has?' I ask, looking towards him and Pops. 'He hasn't said anything.'

I push down another pang of guilt. It hadn't occurred to me that spending so much time with Roscoe meant spending absolutely no time with my family.

'Yeah,' he says. 'He's really good.'

'I don't know how good *I'*ll be,' I say. I'm reminded of just how much I used to enjoy dinner parties and card games. They've been a staple of summer for as long as I can remember; sitting around plastic foldaway tables surrounded by weeping candles, empty bottles and leftovers as we laughed well into the night. It'd be nice to join in, to feel included, again. 'Anyway, I'm just going to . . .' I point over to where Dad and Pops are drying off in the sun.

I drip back over to our sunbeds and take a seat on the edge of my beach towel.

'What were you and Evan talking about?' Pops asks, sliding his sunglasses down.

'Um . . . stuff,' I say. 'Why?'

'I'm just glad to see you're both getting along,' he says. 'He's such a lovely boy.'

I look back at the pool where he's now sitting with a large group of guys; Evan, the popular guy, the guy with the blond beard and bright-blue eyes, the guy who stayed with me when I felt anxious, and I feel my grudge turn to sand.

'Yeah,' I say. 'I suppose he is.'

TWELVE

Monday morning I wake early and untie my paddleboard from the top of the van. Our next campsite is in Saint-Tropez, and I don't know if there'll be a beach nearby that's as good as this one, and I want to give Roscoe a shot on my regular-sized paddleboard since he's struggling with his.

'You look nice,' says Pops, entering the camper-van with an umbrella under his arm.

I screw up my face in the mirror, where I'm trying to brush the knots out of my hair, because I'm wearing my pyjama shorts and an old T-shirt. 'Do I?' I say, looking down at my clothes.

'Fresh,' he says. 'You've caught the sun.'

I turn back to the mirror. My freckles look more pronounced this morning, I guess. The face looking back at me certainly looks different to the one I saw in the bathroom mirror at my therapist's office, which makes me think this summer is starting to do the very thing I wanted it to; it's starting to piece me back together.

'Your dad and I are thinking of driving to Martigues today,' he says. 'It's a place nearby, nicknamed the "Provençale Venice". I can't let that one slip – especially if it's anything like the actual Venice. There's a winery there too – we thought we might stock up for Saint-Tropez.'

'Because there'll be no wine there,' I say sarcastically.

'When it comes to wine, I take no chances,' he says. *'Anyway* – do you fancy it? We can go for lunch somewhere.'

'No, thanks,' I say.

'No?' he repeats.

'I can't go today. I have plans.'

'Oh, right,' he says. 'I'll tell Dad we'll have another beach day then?' He points over his shoulder to outside, where Dad is tying white plastic picnic chairs together.

'No,' I say in a rush.

'No?' he repeats.

'You guys still go. I'm going to go to the beach . . . on my own.'

I look away, keeping my face as still as possible, because Pops has a special talent for reading me and I don't want him to see that I'm lying.

'You'd rather go to the beach *on your own*?' he asks.

'Not *on my own*,' I say, backtracking. 'I mean, I'm . . . meeting friends there.'

'Of course,' says Pops. 'How lovely – who are they? Where are they from?'

'Various places,' I mumble.

'Do they want to come over to the van?' he asks. 'We could have a barbecue tonight. I'll let the Redwoods know—'

'No,' I say, cutting him off. 'I don't want a fuss.'

'Oh,' says Pops, sounding downtrodden. 'I see. Well, your dad and I will still head to Martigues then. The scenery is supposed to be quite special. You'll be OK without us, won't you? You have Julie's number.'

'I'll be fine, Pops,' I say, turning back towards the mirror. 'Go have fun without me.'

I'm way more confident in the sea this time. Without any hesitation I run in, water splashing around me, and submerge myself completely.

'You really are a water baby,' says Roscoe, wading towards me.

I slide on to my board, coming on to my knees when I find my balance. Then I offer him a helping hand so he can join me. I unclip my paddle from its bracket and then twist it through crystalline water, the board gliding effortlessly with every pull. I turn over my shoulder to look at him, at his thick eyelashes and tanned skin. I feel so lucky to be here, floating towards a watercolour horizon, with Roscoe gripping my back. It's kinda everything.

When we're far enough out, I pass him the paddle and then jump into the water, keeping a grip on the side of the board.

'See if you can stand on your knees first,' I say.

'I have done this before,' he replies.

'I'm just trying to help,' I say, holding up my hands.

He pushes forwards and immediately falls on to all fours.

'Knees first, then get on to your feet,' I say. 'It should feel like you're unravelling, bringing your head up last.'

'That's a really cool way of explaining it,' he says. 'Have you ever thought about becoming an instructor?'

'I hadn't,' I say. 'But I think I would actually love a job like that. Especially if it meant living somewhere like this.'

'Could I come and visit you?' he asks, slowly moving on to his feet.

'Of course. I need you to bump unsuspecting tourists off their boards and convince them they need lessons,' I laugh.

'Hey! I don't make a habit of bumping cute tourists off their boards, y'know,' he grins, wobbling slightly.

My heart skips at 'cute'.

'Look – you're doing it!' I say, clapping my hands like a seal.

'I'm paddleboarding!' he shouts. 'I told you it was because of the bigger board. Look at me, world – I'm a paddleboarding ninja!'

He raises the paddle above his head with too much force and the board flies out from under him.

I laugh so hard it actually hurts my throat, and I'm reminded of that day on the pedalo, my favourite summer memory. The laughter is tight and sweet in my stomach, rolling over me in waves.

'Stop!' he says, pulling himself belly first on to the board, his hair a tangle of knots over his face. 'It wasn't that funny.'

'I'm sorry,' I say, my laughter still bouncing in my chest.

'You're still laughing!' he says, and he's laughing too.

'I'm not . . . It was just . . . too . . . funny!'

We fall into hysterics, and I find myself leaning closer into him, my hand resting on his thigh. I swing myself on to the board. 'I don't want to push you into anything you don't feel comfortable with,' I say, picking up the paddle and then moving us back towards the shallows. 'But for the record – that fall was epic.'

'It was an epic fail.' He chuckles behind me.

'Don't do yourself dirty,' I say. 'I said epic *fall* not epic fail. You haven't *failed* at anything.'

As we glide towards the sand, a world of summer, of heat and happiness, around me, I think about how returning to the water was a huge step for me. And it so easily could have gone horribly wrong. I had no idea how I would respond to this, but I'm glad I took the risk. Getting back on my paddleboard again has brought back a part of me I've missed this past year. This person, this Iggy, is who I am; I'm not therapy sessions and sleepless nights and confusion. I'm the kid who loves to play, and swim, the kid who loves to be outdoors. It's crazy how I forgot.

'I didn't realise how much I'd missed boarding,' I say.

'You're really good at it,' he says.

'It isn't even about that,' I say. 'I wouldn't mind if I was terrible at it, it's more about the feeling it gives me. It's like, out here I can breathe again. I can be wholly free. Happy, even.'

'That's . . . awesome,' he says, but there's something about the way he says it.

He goes quiet behind me, and after a minute or so I begin to wonder what he's thinking, where he's gone.

'Is everything OK back there?' I ask.

He doesn't answer right away, but still I wait for him because I'm not the type of person to speak over someone else's thoughts. 'When did you . . . *know*?' he asks.

'Know?' I reply.

'Like, know who you were . . . something you said there, about being wholly free, it made me think . . .'

I don't know if this question would be universally understood, but as a fellow queer kid I know exactly what he's talking about. I think there comes a time in any queer kid's life when they're faced head-on with their identity. For me this sometimes felt tricky, and surprising, and amazing and disappointing and inconsistent, and everything in between, and I can feel Roscoe's need to give a voice to his feelings.

'I knew from an early age that I wasn't like other kids,' I say. 'I only had to look around to see that. I guess, because my parents are gay, we were able to have that conversation pretty early on. It wasn't until recently I realised I was GNC though.'

'GNC?'

'Gender non-conforming.'

'You're lucky,' he says. 'I'm still figuring it out, I think. I know what I think, I know how I feel, but it's not quite as straightforward for me.'

I wait for him to elaborate further, twisting round so we're face to face on the board.

'My parents aren't quite as open,' he says. 'They're great, it's just we can't talk about this kind of stuff, so I haven't had a chance to properly figure it out. I haven't done the whole "coming out" thing yet. All I know is I'm a queer goth kid with a dope new bracelet.'

He holds his wrist in front of my face.

'Oh, you're wearing it?' I say.

'Are you kidding – of course I am!' he says. 'I'll never take it off. Every time I look at it I think of you.'

I touch it, my fingers accidentally brushing his skin, electric needles fizzing in the place where we make contact. I love that he's wearing it. I love that he wants to be reminded of me when I'm not around.

'You're more than a queer goth kid with a dope new bracelet,' I say. 'Never forget it.'

He reaches forward and cups my face, and there's a moment where I think he's going to pull me in closer, maybe even kiss me. My breath catches in my throat. I didn't know until now how much I want that.

He hesitates, looking sideways at the busy beach, his hand going limp on my cheek before he pulls it back. It feels as if the wind has left my sails, like I was riding the crest of a wave and now I've just gone under.

Then he pulls this silly face and topples into the sea headfirst, leaving me floating on my own. And I get this strange feeling; something close to embarrassment or nerves, pressing against my stomach. It's like, there's a moment when he's submerged and I'm *really* on my own, with a beach full of people looking at me. It's so stupid because the sea is still fizzing next to the board, and he'll be back any second, but it's as if I can feel what it's like to be without him. I find myself nervously gripping my hands into fists, my heart all too noticeable in my chest. I don't want this, even for a second.

Which makes me wonder for the first time about the days this summer when we can't see each other at all, and, beyond that, about what's going to happen when we get home.

THIRTEEN

My parents' excitement at the prospect of a child-free day in Saint-Tropez, sipping café au lait in the chicest cafes and shopping in the finest pottery shops the south of France has to offer, is so much that getting away from them is way easier than I thought it was going to be. I mean, I even had a whole PowerPoint presentation planned on my iPad. Turns out I didn't need it.

'You have to keep your phone on loud,' says Pops. 'And call us immediately if anything happens.'

'Nothing's going to happen,' I say.

'Stay safe,' says Dad. 'We won't be going far.'

'I'll be fine,' I say. 'Enjoy your day!'

I kiss them both on the cheek, before I head back into the cobbled streets of the La Ponche quarter, which is the old fishing-village part of town where I'd agreed to meet Roscoe. Pops and Dad have come down to the port to take a look at the many millionaires' yachts that are moored here, their size overshadowing the humble fishing boats that float alongside them, making them look like floating bath toys. As I walk away from them, I can hear Pops cooing at the fabulousness of it all. I think Saint-Tropez might be his favourite place.

I can see why. The town is beautiful, all terracotta buildings with pale blue window shutters, and surprising coves and beaches that seem to appear out of nowhere. The streets are cobbled and narrow, with the smell of buttery pastry flying up to greet me as I make my way past quaint patisserie windows. Though it's a popular destination, Saint-Tropez still manages to hold on to its charming seaside-town status, the air fresh and salty and pecked at by the screeches of hungry seagulls.

Roscoe is exactly where he said he'd be, where we'd planned to meet before we parted ways, in a rocky cove where the historic buildings go right up to the water's edge.

'You're here,' he says, smiling as I approach.

I wrap my arms around him as soon as I'm close enough and we hug.

'It's so good to see you,' I say, my insides dancing like sunlight on water.

'How was your journey?' he asks.

'It was great, actually,' I say. 'It only took a couple of hours.'

We're at the stage in the holiday where Pops and Dad are no longer interested in long drives. Long drives got us to the Med, but now we're here, the longest we'll spend on the road between each place is a couple of hours. We're staying in Saint-Tropez tonight and tomorrow, before we head to Nice. Then it's on to Italy's Ligurian Coast, making our way to our furthest destination, Rome. The exploratory leg of our holiday is always my favourite, and in previous years has taken us to the Swiss Alps, and island hopping across Croatia. But this year things are a little trickier . . .

'What do you want to do today?' I ask.

'I wanted to show you something,' he says. 'It isn't far – we can walk from here.'

We head back into the town, through narrow streets and alleys, until we're back on the water. The coastline Saint-Tropez is built upon juts out into the Mediterranean Sea in a squiggly line, and we follow it until the buildings begin to thin and we're walking along a coastal path; trees and bushes on one side, rocks and sea on the other.

He grabs my hand and pulls me towards him. 'Come on,' he says. 'There's someone I want you to meet.'

We run across the bridge, and then up and down and round, as we navigate the rocky coastal path, weaving in and out of sunlight and through the stretching arms of pine and olive trees.

'Look,' he says, pointing to a gap in the greenery where the trees make way for a garden.

It tumbles down to the water in frilly layers of pink, purple and red. The shrubs around it are well kept, and when the breeze stirs I hear the tin jangling of bells. At the top, past a row of rose bushes, sits an orange-painted house with deep-blue window shutters and a terracotta-tiled roof.

'It's my great-grandmother's house,' he says. 'Would you like to meet her?'

'Seriously?' I ask.

He nods.

'Sure,' I say. 'I'd love to.'

He leads me down some steps where the footpath crosses through a wrought-iron gate. We pass through it into the garden where another set of steps lead us up to the back of the house. There, sitting in the shade of a palm tree, is an old lady on a rocking chair. Though her skin may be creased, and the hair around her face as white as spun sugar, I see the sun shining in her green eyes; *his* eyes.

'Grand-mére Edith,' whispers Roscoe, as we step on to the balcony. 'C'est Roscoe.'

Her face breaks into a smile when she sees him. 'Ah, Roscoe!' she exclaims. Her voice is as bright as water. 'Mon chéri, Roscoe!' She stretches a hand out and he goes to her, taking a seat at her side.

'C'est mon ami, Iggy,' he says, tilting his head towards me.

'Bonjour, Grandma Edith,' I say, taking a step closer.

She smiles at me and then turns back to Roscoe. 'Oh, Roscoe,' she begins. 'Mon enfant chéri. Comme tu me manques. Comme tu me manques.'

'Je suis là,' he whispers. 'I'm here, Grand-mére.'

Her shaking hand squeezes his and she closes her eyes, as if savouring this moment. I notice there are tears in the corners.

'We visited her this morning already,' Roscoe whispers to me. 'But I wanted to steal another moment with her.'

'That's really sweet,' I say.

'I have the fondest memories of coming here,' he says. 'There's a cove just at the bottom of the garden, beyond the footpath. That's where I learnt to swim when I was small. Then just on the other side of that cliff there's a treehouse we used to make the most amazing dens in. I remember one year I left my brother's teddy there, and when I went back it was gone. He cried and cried that night.'

'Mon enfant chéri,' says Grand-mére Edith again. 'Comme tu me manques.'

'I miss you too,' he says, leaning into her and squeezing her hand once more.

It's so lovely to see him with his family, and to hear about his life here. I find myself imagining a young Roscoe playing in the garden, running between the rose bushes and rock jumping in the cove beneath it. And as I do, a memory falls into my head like an apple from a tree. I close my eyes on Saint-Tropez and see something else; I see myself paddleboarding in a quiet cove, which looks exactly like the one at the bottom of the garden. I see the bright water around me, and a feeling of freedom and adventure bouncing around my insides. A warm, tingling sensation scurries up my arms as I think of how happy I was then. I open my eyes, returning to Saint-Tropez and Grand-mére Edith's garden, but the feeling stays. It's then I realise that being here with him brings me the same kind of summer joy that I felt as a kid. He's somehow brought back something that I thought I'd lost, and that I thought I might never find again.

'Qui est là?' calls a voice from inside the house.

I turn to look at Roscoe, who rolls his eyes and sighs. 'Jusqu'à la prochaine fois,' he says, kissing his great-grandma on the cheek, and then he walks over to me. 'Would you like to see the cove?' he asks.

'Yes,' I say.

'Qui est ici?' asks the voice inside the house.

Roscoe steps off the balcony into the garden, and I follow close behind. 'Is there someone else here?' I ask, checking over my shoulder.

'She has a housekeeper,' he says, shrugging. 'She's a bit of a stickler for the rules – we're not supposed to visit during certain times of day. She's supposed to be napping out here. But I know she likes to see me, and I wanted you to meet her. Come on.'

We cross the footpath and down another set of steps until my trainers find the sand. Then he takes my hand and leads me across the beach, all the way to the cliffs on the other side. We make the climb to the top and stand right at the edge. The view is astonishing up here, it's as if we're flying, looking down at a whole world of sparkling blue sea.

'Will you jump with me?' he asks, peering at the water.

'You're not being serious?' I say. It's a long way down.

Jump with me,' he says again, his eyebrows flashing up and down, his face becoming childlike. He tears off his T-shirt, and I stare at his body for a little longer than I should. 'Come on,' he says.

His hand is warm and strong in mine. But as he tugs me forward, I pull back.

I want to be brave. I want to show him I can be just like him, just as carefree. But my knees are locked stiff. It isn't the water; it's the diving, the falling, the letting go. I'm not sure I can. My body is resisting, some part of me still rooted in my past mistake. This is how it happened, isn't it? I carelessly jumped into my biggest mistake without thinking about the consequences. Didn't I?

But, strangely, no memories of diving, or falling come to me.

'Nothing's going to happen,' he whispers, as if reading my thoughts. 'I'm here.'

His words wrap a warm arm around my back, and I feel something slacken. My joints become loose and I'm able to pad from foot to foot at the cliff edge. This isn't last year. This summer couldn't be any further from that, because now I'm not alone; he's here, at my side, like he always will be.

I rip my feet from the earth, like ripping up weeds, and squeeze his hand back.

Then I surrender; we surrender, leaping off the edge of the world as if we could really fly.

The fall is fast and exciting, my belly weightless, my heart sending adrenaline, effervescent in my veins, all the way to my extremities. We hit the water with a thunderous splash, the cold sea shocking against my hot skin.

I feel brave underwater, in the silence. Immediately I reach through the cold for his hand and together we kick to the surface.

The laughter that escapes me bounces around the cove. It's guttural and saccharin and filled with so much summer joy. It's my favourite kind of laughter.

'I did it!' I squeal.

My legs intertwine with his and he grips me closer.

'You did!' he says, his full lips lifting at the edges into a smile.

'I never thought . . .' I begin, 'I mean, after last year and everything . . . that was so awesome!'

'I'm proud of you,' he says.

When he speaks I feel the warmth of his words, the warmth of his breath. We're so close now. Closer than we've ever been, I think. It still isn't close enough.

We swim back towards the beach, and as soon as we hit the sand, we sit side by side at the water's edge, our bodies still intertwined, my head resting on his shoulder. I don't think I've felt happier than I do right now. I don't know if it's because of the adrenaline from the cliff dive, or because there was a time when I genuinely believed I couldn't be happy again, or the way I feel about him, but this moment is all-consuming.

It's strange because I've only known him for a couple of weeks, but I can't imagine *not* knowing him. He's part of me now; we're two of the same, yin and yang, fitting together so perfectly and completely it makes me wonder how I did life without him. Having him here, being so close, is the sweetest thing there is.

I need to know that we're more than a summer thing. I want him in September, and Halloween and Christmas. I want him all year round, not just when the sun shines, and although we have Portofino, and Rome ahead of us, it doesn't seem enough. Now we've made the connection, I don't want to break it when the summer comes to an end, and I want to know if he feels this way too. I want to know if when we get back home we can still be us.

'When will I see you after Rome?' I ask.

'Don't worry about that,' he whispers.

'Just . . . answer the question, Roscoe,' I say, trying to not sound frustrated.

'You can see me whenever you like,' he says. 'Haven't you worked it out by now?' He runs his hands down my arms and pulls me into him, pressing our foreheads together so I'm close enough to feel his hot skin. He closes his eyes and his eyelashes flutter like butterfly wings on his cheeks. I instinctively cup his face in my hands, lifting it so we're nose to nose. My insides begin to spark like flint until my body feels ablaze. I'm no longer myself, I'm heat and tinder and flame, and, perhaps more than anything else, I'm his. He reaches round for the back of my neck and here in the little cove where he spent so many of his childhood summers, sunlight and glass-clear water and whispering breeze, he presses his lips against mine and we kiss.

'I'm crazy about you,' he says, afterwards.

'I miss you already,' I say, closing my eyes.

'We'll be together again soon,' he says, our noses still touching, his thumb stroking my lips.

'What about after that?' I ask.

'Then we'll be together *always*,' he whispers.

FOURTEEN

A few days later the Family Caddock crosses the border into Italy.

As soon as I see the sea, the excitement in my stomach bubbles inside me. I'm meeting Roscoe at a beach called Baia di Paraggi, which isn't too far from Portofino. We decided the town would be too busy and we wanted somewhere a little more intimate. Somewhere just for us.

I've spent the entire night thinking about him and the perfect moment we shared in Saint-Tropez. I can't wait to see him again, feel him again, kiss him again; it's really all I can think about, my blood tingling in fresh places when I do. It was my very first kiss, and to share it with someone as special as him in a place that holds such meaning for him takes everything to the next level. Like, everything had been leading up to *that* moment. It actually surprises me how into this I am. Yeah, I've crushed on people, but this isn't like that. The feelings I have for Roscoe are way more intense because we've made a connection. An actual *real* connection. And there's a chance that this could be something more than late-night fantasies and doodles in sketchbooks.

Maybe this isn't my 'weird girl' era after all; maybe Iggy Caddock is entering their full-on romance era, with gorgeous

European scenery, crashing waves, sunlit kisses, and the cutest, most wonderful guy.

Maybe Iggy Caddock is now a hopeless romantic.

'Where are you going in such a hurry?' Dad asks. We've barely parked the camper-van opposite the Redwoods' before I'm grabbing my beach bag.

'Fancied a full beach day,' I say.

'Which beach?' he asks.

'Um, Baia di Paraggi?' I say.

'Oh, I have such fond memories of last summer at Baia di Paraggi,' says Pops, but then quickly corrects himself. 'Sorry. I didn't mean to say that.'

'It's OK,' I say. 'You're allowed to have good memories about last summer too, you know?'

He nods gently. 'If you give us ten minutes we can lock up the van and come with?'

'No,' I say. 'It's OK.' The last thing I need is my parents being there. That's sure to put a dampener on things. 'I'd like to make some memories of my own.'

I've given it some serious thought and I've decided that I'm going to ask Roscoe if I can tell Dad and Pops about him. I don't want to keep lying to them, and I also *want* them to meet him. I want them to see how happy he makes me. The kiss has taken me to new levels of crushing, to the point where I'm seriously thinking about our future back in the UK, and my parents have to play a part in this.

I know it's only been one kiss, and I know this might be me moving pretty quickly, but that's how things work out here.

People are different on holiday. Life here comes with a time limit. Romances are made and then forgotten as soon as you cross back over the border, and I don't want that to happen. Roscoe and I are so much more than that. I've known this from the moment his paddleboard crashed into mine.

'You don't want your parents cramping your style,' says Dad, tilting his head towards Pops. 'It's OK – we get it. There are plenty of other beaches nearby for us old fogies to go to, or we might pop into Portofino, it isn't far. You go and enjoy your freedom, Iggs.'

The sun is hot as I crunch along the sandy footpath, through crisp branches and clawing plants. The Italian Riviera already feels different to the French one, hotter and made of harder edges, but the beach is still beautiful. I look up at either side of the cove to see cliffs with twisting lemon trees growing on their backs and a sea that is as smooth as a millpond. I go to the water's edge, allowing the cool water to wash over my feet as my toes sink out of sight into the sand. The waves whisper to me to close my eyes, to shut off all other distractions so I can wholly be here in this summer moment.

'Hey.'

I'm a wild thing now; I'm hot sun and salt, sea and sand. The breeze brushes Roscoe against my skin, bringing with it the smell of his hair, his shirt, his skin.

'Hey, you,' I say.

I throw my arms around him, and he holds me close, my hands pressed against his strong back. Then, taking my hand, he leads me along the water's edge to where a guy is sitting next to a handful of rowing boats.

'These seem easier than a paddleboard,' he says, nudging my side. 'What do you reckon?'

'Oh, fun!' I say.

The guy reels off a few safety instructions before sliding the boat into the water, and just like that it's ours for the morning. I pick up the oars and row us into deeper water, the sun poking through the trees and warming my back. I row until we're just past the cliffs, where the breeze brings with it the smell of sea salt and lemon groves, and then stop so we can float among the breathtaking Italian scenery.

Roscoe is wedged into the bow, peering over the edge, the light reflecting off the water highlighting the bends and grooves of his face, and I think there might be only one thing more beautiful than the Italian coastline.

'You're . . . very special,' I say.

'I am?' he asks.

'You're not like anybody else,' I say. 'I . . . didn't know guys could be like you.'

'OK. Please elaborate.'

'It's just – you make me feel happy in ways I'd never thought about before.'

'You make me feel happy too,' he says.

'No, it's more than that,' I say. 'You *see* me. You embrace everything that I am, and it even makes me love myself that little bit more.'

'That's beautiful,' he says. 'I'm so glad I make you feel that way.'

I want to get closer to him, want to be kissing him, but I don't know how to ask for that. Does that sound strange? He looks at me and I have to look away. I don't want him to see that I'm being weird right now.

'I might swim,' I say, staring at the water, the edges of my eyes stinging from its brightness.

'Of course you will, water baby,' he says. 'I knew it wouldn't take long.'

The little boat wobbles from side to side as we stand, and then we're diving into another world, a world of blue and green, of slowed down and heavy, a world that's different, and yet somehow part of this one.

The sound of summer, of distant jet skis and waves and beach bars, disappears. Underwater, there is only silence. We move like dancers; twirling and spinning and flipping as one. We swim even deeper, where the water turns cold and crabs cling to rocks, and it feels like we're the only two people in the world.

As we finally break the surface a school of flying fish whizz past, leaping from the water above our heads, some coming so close I feel them skim my nose.

I scream.

'A water baby who's scared of fish?' Roscoe laughs as we climb back into the boat.

'*Flying* fish,' I specify, but I can't help but laugh too. 'And it's not that they're fish, it's that they came out of nowhere.'

'Look,' he says. In his hand he's holding a white shell, twisting and pointy. It looks exactly like the one from my bag. 'I found treasure!'

'You're too cute.' I smile.

'For you,' he says, pressing the shell into my palm. My heartbeat thunders in my ears. Our knees are touching and he begins to stroke my leg, his index finger brushing up and down my skin. I feel the hairs stand on end as if there's electricity in my veins.

'You're not like anybody else either,' he whispers, leaning in, his lips parting mine.

We move together, our mouths finding each other's in perfect symmetry. As if they were always meant to lock together in this way. As if *we* were always meant to lock together in this way. His lips touch mine and I taste the salt of the sea. I gently bite him, and he cups my face in his hands. The kiss deepens. I close my eyes so I can truly lose myself in this moment, in his mouth, in his touch and his warmth. Suddenly, Baia di Paraggi disappears and I'm transported somewhere else. Somewhere dark. No longer do I hear Roscoe's breath or his heart pounding against my own. Instead, I hear laughter, as sharp as a knife.

There's a group of guys not too far away. Their laughter rings in my ears, presses against my eyes and forehead and throat. I'm scared, but I don't want to show it. I don't want them to think I'm weak.

Then I'm running. But the laughter chases me through a forest, over uneven ground where branches and vines tear at my skin, but I have to keep going. I have to keep moving forwards.

There's a river ahead. The water glows red, mirroring the light of the setting sun like a blood-stained blade. I scream. I can't go back. If I go back, they'll kill me. I know it. I have no choice. I go into the water . . .

'*Iggy?*' Roscoe asks.

I'm back on the boat, floating on a calm sea after the tempest of my memory, their laughter still slicing through me. Why did our kiss trigger something so dark?

'Are you OK?'

'I'm . . . Did you hear that?' I ask, shaking the remnants away.

'Hear what?' he asks.

'The noise,' I say, looking back at the beach.

Most of my memories return to me broken; they come back to me out of shape and with missing pieces. But this memory came to me more whole and more complete than all of the others, with so many feelings attached.

'What noise?' he asks.

'Laughing,' I say. *It was clear as day*, I think.

'Laughing?' he asks. 'Who was laughing? There's nobody around.'

The memory is already flying away from me. I try to chase it, running in the dark through the twists and turns of my mind, but it's too quick for me, like a firefly flittering away.

'It . . . doesn't matter,' I say, reaching out to stroke his leg. I kiss him again but his lips don't move.

'You look like you've seen a ghost,' he says. 'Are you sure you're OK?' His finger brushes a stray hair behind my ear, his other hand cupping my head.

I think about telling him. But I'm still straddling two places, and I need time to think, and this time, our time, is too precious for that. 'I'm good,' I say, forcing a smile. 'You don't need to worry about me.'

The lie leaves a coppery taste in my mouth, like blood.

FIFTEEN

It always strikes me as strange that Pops brings his art stuff on holiday. Oil paints and easels are a big part of his job, and I'd have thought he'd be happy to leave them behind. But there comes a time every summer when Pops' hand itches to hold a paintbrush again. Tonight he sits outside the camper-van, his easel backing on to the end of our row of pitches and the olive grove beyond, with the most beautiful scarlet sky above, smeared with heavy strokes of orange and pink. I step down on to the gravel and take a peek over his shoulder. For a moment it's hard to see where the painting finishes and the sky begins.

Dad is sitting next to the Redwoods' camper-van with Dave Redwood, drinking bottles of Italian beer. There doesn't seem to be anybody else around; the night is quiet, when it would usually be filled with communal barbecues, and poker games over flickering citronella candles.

'Where is everybody?' I ask.

'Coach trip to Portofino,' Pops replies, not looking up from his canvas. 'We got back a little earlier. If you're hungry there are fresh tomatoes, ham and cheese in the fridge.'

'I'm not hungry,' I lie.

This time he does look at me.

'You need to eat something, Iggy,' he says. 'You know what you're like – you won't sleep tonight if you don't.'

I don't think I'm going to sleep tonight anyway, I think.

He makes three broad strokes on the canvas before putting his brush down.

'OK,' he says, turning to face me. 'What's happened?'

'Nothing,' I mumble.

'It doesn't look like nothing,' he says. 'Come on – you know you need to talk about things when you're feeling overwhelmed. It's no good bottling it up. Did something happen at the beach today?'

I begin to nod, slowly at first but then stronger as Pops' words echo in my head. *I need to talk. It's no good bottling it up.*

'I . . . remembered something,' I begin. 'About last year.'

'Oh, love,' he says. 'What was it?'

'I . . . I remembered why I went into the river. I was . . . running from someone. Maybe more than one person. They chased me to the river and I had no choice but to try and cross. I was . . . so scared . . .'

Pops' face grows paler, his eyes wide as he watches me. 'Why were they chasing you, Iggy?' he asks.

'I don't know,' I whisper. 'I wish I could remember that part, but I can't. All I know is that I didn't go in the water because I wanted to; I went in because I *had* to. And that changes things. I mean, doesn't it?'

'Changes things how?'

'It means it wasn't my fault.'

This makes his mouth drop open, makes him stand, makes

him walk over to my side. 'Of course it wasn't your fault,' he says, pulling me into him. 'How could you think that?'

I don't know, I think. I've been carrying something around with me for a year, something that's felt unbearably heavy at times, but I didn't realise until now that it was guilt. Guilt about what happened, about what I put my family through. Guilt that Dad and Pops spent months worried and stressed and overtired. Guilt that they argued so much during that time. I'd thought it was my fault. I'd thought I made the stupid decision that had caused so much disruption to our lives. But I didn't. Someone else had made that decision for me. I can't believe it.

'Have you been blaming yourself for all of this time?' asks Pops.

I nod.

'Oh, my darling,' he says, squeezing me tighter. 'You have to be kind to yourself. You went through something so scary last year, and it's going to take time.'

'I don't want it to take time,' I snap. 'I don't want this hanging over my head forever. I want to be normal.'

I don't want such incredible moments, like kissing Roscoe, to be stolen away from me because of something that happened a year ago. I don't want to be triggered when I'm enjoying myself because I'm being controlled by something that I don't understand. It seems more answers only bring more questions, and I'm wondering where it's going to end. I know my monster is here, but I don't know it's shape, or size. How am I supposed to be brave and face up to something as elusive as that? How am I supposed to face something that not only attacks me in the dark, but in the light of day too? That seems like an impossible task. Is this all I have to look forward to for the rest of summer? Will even the sweetest moments be soured by my past?

I stand, pushing my chair away, frustration boiling up inside me.

'Where are you going?' asks Pops.

'I need to clear my head,' I say, stalking away from him.

'Iggy – it's late,' he shouts behind me.

But I don't turn back; don't even acknowledge he's spoken. There's only one person I want to see now, one person who can make these messy feelings go away, one person who understands me.

I find him sitting on the wall by the entrance of the campsite, his legs folded beneath him as he bites at the skin down the side of his thumbnail.

I take a seat next to Roscoe, deflating on to the wall, my shoulders and arms hanging forward heavily. I don't know what to say. I don't know where to start. So we sit in silence, watching the coach from Portofino as it growls past us, turning slowly into the campsite. I hear it hissing to a stop, the doors flipping open and tired voices spilling out.

'I remembered something today,' I say. 'While we were in the boat.'

'Was it about the accident?' he asks gently.

I nod. 'Pops just tried to talk to me about it,' I say. 'But what's the point, right? I mean, he doesn't know what this is like. Nobody does.'

'I'm sure he's only trying to help,' he says.

'But he can't help,' I say. 'That's the whole point – I can't *be* helped. I'm alone in this.'

'You're not alone.'

'I need to know what happened,' I say. 'I know you think that I should be joyful in every moment, and that it's easy, but it isn't. I need answers. Truth comes before joy and I need to know why I was running and who I was running from.'

He looks just like Pops did only moments ago. He looks just how everybody looks at me now, because I'm a fragile thing, wading through my broken memories alone.

'Remembering isn't going to be easy, Iggy,' he says. 'You have to realise that the more you dig, the harder this is going to get.'

'I need to know,' I say, shaking my head. I can't have the mystery, can't be forever pursued by a monster I don't know the shape of.

It might seem to him and everyone else that I'm pressing some sort of imaginary self-destruct button, but I'd rather know the truth than delude myself with a lie. Lies are unstable and changeable, and I can't build a future on either of these things. I need the truth. That's what this holiday was supposed to be about.

Roscoe stands, stretching his arms above his head. 'I need to get back,' he says. 'We're leaving in the early hours of the morning.'

I feel like a rock has landed in my stomach. The next time I'll see him is in three days and that feels like forever away. I'm not sure I can be without him for that long.

'Are we still meeting at the Trevi Fountain on the fifteenth?' I ask, as brightly as I can.

'There's nowhere else I'd rather be,' he says.

He leans forward and kisses me, our lips finding each other, finding their natural place again, and for a moment everything else goes away.

'I wish it could be like this all the time,' I whisper. 'I wish we could be together all of the time.'

'It doesn't work like that,' he says, kissing me again.

'I miss you already,' I say.

'You'll see me soon,' he says. He holds out his little finger. 'Pinky promise.'

Our fingers entwine and he pulls me in for another kiss.

And then he's gone.

'Goodbye, Roscoe,' I whisper.

'Who are you talking to?' someone asks behind me.

I look over my shoulder to see Evan Redwood watching me, as if he's been watching me for a while.

'Nobody,' I say.

He's carrying a gift-shop bag in his hand and has his maroon backpack on his back.

'How was Portofino?' I ask.

'Was there somebody here just now?' he asks, ignoring my question.

'What? Yeah. But he's gone.'

'He?'

I don't answer him, just nod before hurrying past, but he stays right behind me, like a shadow. We crunch along the dimly lit path until we get to the end of our road, but before I can turn on to it I feel his hand grip my elbow.

'*Who?*'

'What?'

'Who were you talking to?' he asks again, pulling me towards him.

'Evan, get off me,' I say, snatching my arm back. 'Stop being weird.'

'Why won't you answer?' he says.

'Why are you so bothered?' I say.

'Just answer the question—'

'No! Who I hang around with has absolutely nothing to do with you. I don't owe you anything, Evan, and I don't have to answer your question. OK?'

Julie Redwood is sitting outside our camper-van, sharing a bottle of red wine with Pops.

'Oh, hi, Iggy,' she says. 'How was Baia di Paraggi?'

'It was nice, thanks,' I say. 'Pretty.'

I dive past them towards the camper-van door because I'm not in the mood for socialising this evening.

'Aren't you going to ask Julie about Portofino?' Pops asks pointedly.

'Where did you disappear to, Evan?' asks Julie.

I turn round to see him standing by the table, looking at me. No – *staring* at me.

'I just bumped into Iggy,' he begins. 'It's getting dark, so I thought I'd walk them back.'

'How thoughtful of you,' says Pops. 'Isn't that thoughtful, Iggy?'

'Sure,' I say, but it comes out as more of a sigh than a word.

I pull the door towards me, and I'm just about to climb the

steps inside when Evan says, 'They were sitting on the wall outside the campsite, talking to someone.'

I turn round slowly, meeting him dead in the eye.

'Oh,' says Pops, placing his wine glass down on to the table. 'I thought you'd gone for a walk to clear your head.'

'I did,' I say.

'So who did you meet?' he asks.

'Just . . . a friend,' I say.

'They won't tell me who,' says Evan.

'Because it's none of your business!' I snap.

'Iggy,' says Pops sternly.

'Well, it isn't,' I say.

As I look at Evan, I begin to wonder if trusting him, if believing in this personality transplant of his, has been wise. People don't change. Not that much. In this moment I'm seeing glimpses of the boy I once knew, and it's messing with my head. 'It's been a long day,' I say. 'Can't I just go to bed?'

Pops looks at me for longer than is comfortable. It isn't totally clear what he's thinking. Usually his feelings are painted all over his face, as if smeared over one of his blank canvases. But tonight I can't tell if he's concerned or just plain annoyed.

I look at the ground and eventually he says, 'Fine. We don't need to talk about this now. Say goodnight to Julie and Evan.'

'Goodnight, Julie and Evan,' I mumble, before climbing into the camper-van and closing the door behind me.

SIXTEEN

The memory of the river plays on my mind for the next couple of days as we pack up our things and move to our next destination, a campsite just outside the city of Pisa. It's thrown me, and not just because of what the memory showed me, but the way it crept up on me so suddenly. I didn't think memories could do that. I didn't realise how susceptible to my trauma I still am. I thought that I'd left the worst of it behind the day I walked out of the hospital in Dijon, but, clearly, I was wrong.

I keep a low profile, moping by myself in the camper-van. The Redwoods haven't joined us on this campsite; they've headed a little further east to visit Florence, so it's not even as if I'm avoiding Evan. I should be out there in the world, soaking up the sunshine and living my best kind of summer. I should be happy to be just us, to have my parents to myself, but without Roscoe I'm finding happy a little tough at the moment.

I think about him a lot. I miss him. I realise this more with every passing hour. He's made this holiday magical in ways I didn't know holidays could be, and now he's not here I'm realising that I need his special brand of magic all of the time. At night I can't find sleep, no matter how fiercely I try. I wriggle my toes, and scratch my back, and toss from one side of the bed to the other, the camper-van moving with me, but still I can't do anything but lie among the moonlight and cricket song and heat as I think of him. By day I'm distracted, sitting at the breakfast table locked inside my head as Pops and Dad talk about the galleries and museums they want to visit in Italy, or fancy restaurant recommendations they've been given in Rome. I can't hear a word of it. I wonder what he's doing. I wonder where he is. I wonder if I'm playing as big a part in his holiday as he is in mine. I wonder if, right now, he's thinking about me, like I am him . . .

'*Iggy*,' says Pops, snapping me out of my daydream and bringing me back to the breakfast table. 'Did you hear what I just said?'

'Sorry,' I say. 'I'm tired – didn't sleep too well last night.'

Roscoe has quite literally turned my life upside down, where dreaming happens in the daytime and at night I'm at my most awake.

'We know,' yawns Dad.

The problem with having a sleepless night in a camper-van is that everybody else has a sleepless night too.

'Sorry,' I say again.

I reach forward and tear the crusty end of a croissant, pastry tumbling on to the plate like confetti. I put it in my mouth and try to chew what tastes like flavourless dust, before quickly swallowing and placing it back down.

'Are you feeling well?' asks Pops, touching the back of his hand to my forehead.

'I'm fine,' I say, flinching away from him. 'Just tired.'

He looks at me suspiciously and I can't look back at him; if I do, he'll know what I'm thinking. He'll see that my thoughts are all about Roscoe, a boy he doesn't know anything about, and then he'll have questions – more than he already does – and I'm bad at lying, especially to him.

'How do we feel about a day in Pisa?' asks Dad, changing the subject. 'You'd love it, Iggy – there's obviously the famous leaning tower, but also some fabulous places to eat, and—'

'I'm staying here,' I say, quickly claiming my ground.

I just want it to be Rome now so I can see him again. I don't need Pisa, or leaning towers or fabulous places to eat. I just want him.

'How do you *really* feel, Iggs?' asks Dad sarcastically.

'Don't you want to see the tower?' asks Pops. 'We've never been here before. It's supposed to be fabulous.'

'I'm good,' I say, shaking my head.

'What would you do instead?' asks Pops.

'Just stay here,' I say. He screws up his face, as he undoubtedly wonders why someone would want to stay cooped up in a warm camper-van when they could be out exploring one of the most beautiful places in Italy.

'But you'd be on your own,' he says.

'I'll be OK,' I say. 'I was OK in Saint-Tropez, wasn't I? You can trust me.'

'I know we can,' says Pops, nodding. 'It isn't that. I would just feel terrible if—'

'Nothing is going to happen,' I say. I mean it literally, because all I'm going to do is sit here and fantasise. That's it.

'Julie and Dave aren't even here to help you out,' he says. 'What if you get hungry?'

'Then I'll make myself a sandwich.' I understand their concern as Pisa is a little further away from this campsite than Baia di Paraggi, or the beach in Provence, but they need to cut me some slack. 'Look, I'm fine on my own. I'm sixteen – I'm practically an adult.'

'You're not,' says Dad.

'I *so* am!' I protest. 'I'm old enough to do stuff on my own. In fact, I *enjoy* doing stuff on my own. Like, I was fine going to the beach back in France. I'll be fine here on my own. I'd even rather go to Rome on my own.'

'You want to go to Rome on your own?' asks Dad.

'No. I mean, yeah – I quite fancy exploring Rome on my own.' Saying it out loud definitely sounds stranger to how it sounded inside my head. 'I'm old enough to do that.'

Pops looks at me suspiciously over the top of his sunglasses. 'You do realise that the campsite is on the outskirts of the city,' he says. 'Rome is a good hour away from where we're staying.'

'Forty-five minutes by train,' I say. 'I googled it.'

'You want to go on a forty-five-minute train journey, in Italy, on your own?' asks Dad.

I nod, trying to pull the sweetest face I can, which used to work when I was twelve. I'm not convinced it's going to this time.

'Out of the question,' says Dad, shaking his head.

'But—'

'We'll think about it,' says Pops, raising his hands to stop the imminent argument from breaking out.

'You . . . you will?' I ask.

'We will?' asks Dad at the same time.

'Yes,' Pops says. 'You've respectfully made a request, and we'll think about it.'

Without needing a prompt from me, my mind shows me an imaginary montage of Roscoe and me in Rome, walking through the ancient streets hand in hand, maybe even sharing a kiss by some fabulous landmark.

'This is awesome,' I whisper.

'We haven't said yes yet,' says Dad.

'I know,' I say. 'But you haven't said no either.'

The night before we leave, Pops calls a family meeting around the camp table.

'We've thought about your request,' he says. 'And we've decided to allow you some independent time in Rome.'

'*You have?*' I say. I really didn't know which way this was going to go. I was hopeful, sure, but Pops can be quite strict when he wants to be. But then I remember that he's different here; Holiday Pops is much more chill than Home Pops.

'Yes,' he says. 'Also, we thought we might stay in a hotel for the night. We want to be able to enjoy the Eternal City without a time limit.'

'That's . . . incredible!' I say, gripping my hands into fists. Being able to go off on my own to meet Roscoe is amazing on so many levels, but staying in a hotel too means even *more* time with him. This has turned out better than I could have hoped.

'Thanks, Pops!' I squeal.

The montage in my mind begins to play again. I see Roscoe and me meeting at the Trevi Fountain – stealing a moment to throw a coin into the water and make a wish, walking over the

Tiber River as the sun sets behind Castel Sant'Angelo, and stopping for an ice cream on the Spanish Steps. And that's where we'll finally plan how we're going to see each other back in the UK. It's in Rome, in the Eternal City, that we'll make an eternal promise to each other, sealed with a kiss. I can feel it.

'What about me?' asks Dad. 'I had some part in this too, you know.'

'Thanks, Dad,' I say, beaming at him.

'Of course, there is one condition,' says Pops.

'Anything,' I say. 'Name your price.'

'We're putting a lot of trust in you, Iggy,' he continues. 'We expect you to behave safely and responsibly . . .'

'Done!' I say.

'. . . and, though we're prepared to let you go off without us, we don't want you to be completely alone, and so we'll let you go as long as you take Evan with you.'

'No,' I say. It's out before I even have time to stop it.

'Iggy—' Pops begins.

'You can't be serious?' I ask.

The movie in my mind stops playing, as if someone has just unplugged the Wi-Fi. My mind goes blank so quickly I don't even have a chance to take one final glance at the magic, and the sunset and Roscoe – perhaps the most beautiful of it all – before it's gone.

'I'm deadly serious,' says Pops. 'Julie and I have planned a gorgeous lunch in a taverna near the Trevi Fountain, and so while we're eating, you both can—'

'No!' I say again, this time more firmly. They can't do this to me. I won't allow it. I don't need a chaperone. And I certainly don't need Evan Redwood to be a third wheel. No way. It's not happening.

'Iggy,' says Dad.

'You can't do this to me. I'm sixteen – I'm not a child. I don't need Evan. I don't need anybody!'

'Can you calm down, please,' says Dad.

'Sixteen is not old enough to go off on your own,' says Pops.

'But – it's only for an afternoon, and I'll have my phone with me, and you can track it, and—'

'It's not happening, Iggy,' says Pops. 'We've said you can go explore without parental supervision, and I think taking a friend is a small price to pay. Also, I think it's terribly kind of Evan to agree to go with you when you're so rude to him most of the time. We're not going to let you just wander off on your own in somewhere as busy as Rome. You'll be safer with Evan and—'

'But why *him*?' I ask.

'Because Julie and Dave will be joining us for lunch, and we thought you two would like to go and explore together.'

'You thought wrong,' I mutter.

'Well, that's the best you're going to get, Iggy,' says Pops, standing suddenly. He begins to clear our dinner plates from the table, stacking them together noisily and dumping the cutlery on top. I don't know what he has to be so annoyed about; it isn't his life that's just been ruined. 'Take it or leave it. You either come with us, or you go and explore Rome with Evan. The choice is yours.'

SEVENTEEN

At first glance, Rome doesn't seem all that different to many of the other European cities we've visited. But then we take a short taxi ride from the railway station to the hotel, and I see the mixture of the romantic and the ancient, effortlessly pieced together under a crisp blue sky, and I realise that there is nothing quite like Rome.

We knew it was ambitious to try and fit it into the holiday, and there was a huge chance that we simply wouldn't have the time or energy left, but, as I see the magnificent ring-like Coliseum – like the remains of a giant ancient birthday cake from a party that ended a very long time ago – and the gleaming white marble of the monument to Victor Emmanuel II, I'm so glad we did.

The hotel is on a side street not too far from the Trevi Fountain. I'm meeting Roscoe there this afternoon at five o'clock. I can't wait to see him. I know it's only been three days, but it feels so much longer.

I've thought about what I want to say to him. Rome is his last destination too. After here, he flies back to the UK. And then? Are we going to be more than a holiday fling? Dare I believe that we keep this going back home? I know that I'd like that. I guess today will be all about finding out if he does too. I'd be lying if I said a certain element of doubt hadn't crept in.

Another obstacle I have to contend with today, as well as my own self-doubt, is Evan. He purposefully sat opposite me on the train, and I purposefully listened to music the entire journey so I wouldn't have to engage with him. I've given it some thought, and I've decided I'm going to ask him if I can have some time on my own today. Rome is a big place, and I don't want him to feel overwhelmed, but at the same time, he simply can't be there when I meet Roscoe. We have a pass until eight o clock as, after lunch, our parents are visiting some gallery in the city, so I'm going to ask if we can go our separate ways for a bit around five o clock, so I can make my way to the Trevi Fountain, and he can do the things he wants to do. Surely he'll be happy about this? He can't want to spend the entire day making awkward conversation.

As soon as I open the taxi door, the dry heat presses against my skin. We've clung to the coast all summer, and so, though it's been hot, the Mediterranean Sea air has kept us fresh. There is no sea air in Rome. Actually, it feels like there's no air in Rome at all. Heat beats down from the sky and rises from the pavements, leaving us in a thick heat pocket in the middle.

After check-in, we take our bags up to the room. It's nice, with air conditioning and a black balustrade outside the window. I sink on to the bed, bouncing up and down a few times to test its squishiness; it's been a long time since I've slept in a proper bed.

As I unpack my yellow rucksack, something catches my eye. I rarely use the front pocket, but poking out of the top, caught in the zip, is the corner of a postcard. I dive in, my fingertips brushing against Black Sea sand that sticks under my fingernails, and then, gripping its edges, I pull it out. It's from Provence: I would recognise the beige rocks and aquamarine sea anywhere. Nowhere else has a coastline like in the south of France. I turn it over in my hands and see the back is covered in writing, words crawling on their sides on scribbled legs up the edges. But it's the name signed at the bottom that catches my attention first.

Roscoe

He must have slipped it into my bag when we took the boat out in Baia di Paraggi.

The sigh that leaves me sounds sweeter than any sigh I've made before, as if the air it floats upon is made of spun sugar. He must have known how much I've wanted to hear from him these past three days.

I begin to read, inhaling every single one of his words as quickly as I can:

Iggy aka my water baby,

This isn't actually a postcard from Provence. Well. It is, because it's a postcard with 'Provence' written on it, and there's a picture of a place that I'm assuming is also in Provence on the front, but I need to stop wasting space writing about this. I want you to know that I'm really looking forward to seeing you. I'll be thinking of you every second of every day until we're together again. Meeting you has been the single most unexpected thing that has ever happened to me. I never thought I'd meet someone as wonderful as you on holiday this year. You are magic in human form to me, and I can't wait to be with you again.

Roscoe

My eyes feel wet at the edges. I feel the most joyful I may have ever felt in my life, but still my eyes are warm and damp. These are the nicest words anybody has ever written to me, and the fact that he hid this postcard in my bag, knowing I'd be surprised when I found it, only makes this moment all the more special. With this postcard he's taken away all of my doubts. Everything I was getting in my head about – about how we'd make it work back in the UK, and whether he even wanted to – have been eradicated with these words scribbled in blue ink. This is tangible proof that he cares about me, that we are more than simply a summer romance.

I hold the warm bending card to my chest, and sigh a quiet 'thank you'.

'How's your room, Iggs,' asks Dad, poking his head round the door.

'Um, nice,' I say, sliding the postcard under my arm. 'It's lovely, actually.'

'I'm looking forward to a night away from the old van,' he chuckles.

'Me too,' I say.

He grips the doorframe as if he's about to leave, but then he hesitates for a moment, taking a little longer to look at my face.

'You look very spritely,' he says. 'What's that you have in your hand?'

'Oh, it's nothing,' I say.

His face twists, sitting somewhere between questioning and surprised, and I can't help but laugh.

'What's so funny?' he asks.

'Oh, just . . . Rome.' I smile.

After a quick costume change, we meet everyone in the hotel lobby.

Pops and Dad look so smart. They're both wearing freshly ironed shirts, one blue, the other white, and Pops is wearing a cream fedora and sunglasses. The types of holidays we go on never call for freshly ironed shirts and fedoras. As I steal a sideways glance at them, looking all happy and suntanned, standing holding hands in the hotel lobby, I feel a burst of happiness on my insides. Rome looks good on them.

'Now, look after each other,' says Pops as I step on to the polished floor. 'And keep your phone on loud.'

'And call us straight away if anything happens,' says Julie.

'It's very hot out there today,' says Dad. 'Don't forget to drink plenty of water – I've put a fresh bottle in your bag. And use plenty of sun cream.'

'We'll be fine,' says Evan, chuckling. 'Go and enjoy your fancy lunch.'

Pops pulls me closer and kisses the side of my forehead. 'Have a gorgeous day, my darling,' he says.

'You too, Pops,' I say.

'Bye, Iggs,' says Dad, kissing my cheek. 'Call us if you need us.'

'You'd think we were going away for a month,' says Evan jokingly.

This actually makes me laugh.

As soon as our parents are gone, we make our way out of the hotel on to the busy road outside.

'Where do you want to go first?' asks Evan.

Considering how much I've been thinking about this day, it comes as a surprise that I haven't given much thought to what Evan and I are actually going to do. In my mind's eye, my day in Rome was going to be spent with Roscoe, but the reality is I'll be spending more of it with Evan.

'The Trevi Fountain is nearby,' he says. 'We could start there and then work our way down to the Pantheon?'

'Oh, no,' I say assertively. 'How about we go straight to that Pantheon place?' He tilts his head to the side. 'The Trevi Fountain is so close to the hotel – it seems like a nice place to end,' I lie.

'Right,' he says, nodding slowly. 'I guess that makes sense. The Pantheon it is then.'

The roads of Rome look as if they're melting, with the stones beneath our feet curved and shiny as we make our way through winding streets, Evan leading the way with his iPhone held in his hand. As we walk down the alleyway from our hotel, I keep my chin up so I can take it all in. There's magic in this city. It comes at you right from the front, exciting all of your senses at the same time: beauty, lights, smells and sounds, every corner is an event. Nothing is left to chance. A simple table holding a single candle on a cobbled alleyway is enough, or a water fountain here, or a balustrade there. It's like Rome knows how monumental it is; it doesn't need to try.

Before we even reach the Pantheon, the Temple of Hadrian surprises us suddenly; it looks so decrepit, but also monumental and strong at the same time.

'He's an interesting character, Hadrian,' says Evan, as we walk by. 'He and his lover, Antinous, are probably the most famous gay couple in Roman history.'

I find this comment a little surprising coming from Evan Redwood. Who knew he was so invested in queer Roman history?

Next is the Pantheon, where Evan takes about fifty pictures. We even take a selfie together, which he posts on Instagram. I never thought I'd see the day where a picture of us makes his grid, but there we are, standing outside the historical landmark as if we were always meant to explore the city together, as if we're real holiday friends. Then it's the magnificent Piazza Navona, where we stop for ice cream.

'I feel like I'm on a film set,' I say, as I take pictures of the marble statues that sit around the huge needle-like column in the middle of the square, water springing from their feet.

I get chocolate gelato and Evan gets two scoops of strawberry cheesecake. It's a messy affair in the heat; I have streams of chocolate down my hands, and even some on my wrist. As soon as I wipe one away, another races behind it.

There are artists dotted around the square. Some draw the scenery while others offer to sketch portraits of couples, and I feel sad that I'm not seeing all of this for the first time with Roscoe.

Although, Evan isn't nearly as annoying as I thought he would be. Usually when Evan and I are forced together like this, the awkwardness is palpable, like there's an elephant in the room, but Rome is so grand and obnoxious it feels like it's taken on the role of the elephant so we don't have to worry about it, we can just enjoy the experience.

'I wonder how our parents are enjoying their fancy lunch,' I say, as we look down on the foundations of a Roman relic, where all of the city's cats have gathered.

'I'm sure the red wine is flowing,' says Evan. 'Oh, this is the place where Julius Caesar was assassinated.' His face lifts with excitement. 'History tells us he was stabbed by his once friend, Brutus, which is why people associate this name with betrayal. There was a theatre here.' He points at a circle of crumbling columns. 'I'm guessing that's it.'

I try to imagine it in its heyday, thousands of years ago. It looks pretty impressive now and so I can only imagine what it must have looked like back then. Rome really is full of surprises. It's only been a couple of hours, but already I've seen more ancient monuments than I have in my entire life. Not to mention tasted the best gelato ever.

'You're really into Roman history,' I say. It's something I didn't know about him. Actually, today I'm seeing a side of him that up until now I never would have dreamed existed. 'What can you tell me about Julius Caesar?' I ask, because I can tell he's dying to.

'I like history in general,' he says. 'It was always my favourite subject. I don't actually know that much about Caesar; I know he was a dictator, I know he was assassinated, I know he, supposedly, had a son with Cleopatra . . .'

'As in the Egyptian goddess?' I interrupt.

'Well, she wasn't a goddess,' he says.

'But she was fabulous, so . . . I'm sticking with goddess,' I say.

'OK,' he chuckles. 'Anyway, what else do I know? They named a month after him – July – which is crazy because we still call it that today.'

'That *is* crazy,' I say. 'Why did they assassinate him if they liked him enough to name a month after him?'

'He got too powerful, I think.' He shrugs.

'That old chestnut,' I mutter.

We emerge from the city streets on the bank of the river, which lazes beneath us like a giant green snake, moving slowly in the heat. On the other side I see the climbing turrets of Castel Sant'Angelo, and the bridge with statues on it in front.

'It's mad how green the water is,' I say. 'It looks like a countryside river.'

Reeds push up in the shallows, where ducks and moorhens float and dive beneath the surface. I didn't think city rivers could look like this. The only city rivers I've seen have been brownish and industrial looking; the Tiber is softer than that, with a smooth surface and greenery and muddy marshland sitting alongside the ancient stone banks.

There are crowds of people down here, gathered in groups, eating and chatting and playing music. We decide to take a break and join them, sitting in the shade of a nearby tree.

Evan tells me about the castle, and I'm yet again surprised about how knowledgeable he is about Roman history, offering up interesting facts here and there about the architecture or long-gone emperors. Maybe it's because we're older now, and a little more mature, but I feel like I'm actually *enjoying* his company.

We bask in the afternoon sun by the river, Evan playing music on his phone, and I enjoy feeling so chill. It's the perfect headspace to be in to meet Roscoe later. I actually don't feel so bad about leaving Evan now that I know he likes Rome so much. I imagine he'd love to explore for a couple of hours on his own.

'Where else would you like to visit today?' I ask him, when the time on my phone creeps towards four thirty. I'm meeting Roscoe at five, and I have to somehow find the Trevi Fountain again.

'Hmmm,' he says, pursing his lips. 'I'd like to properly see the Coliseum. And I'd quite like to visit St Peter's Square too.'

'OK,' I say. 'Well – there are some other places I'd like to see too, so how do you feel about doing our own thing for a few hours?'

I lift my face into the broadest smile I can, as if I'm talking to a toddler who's just thrown his toys out of the pram, and I need to get him onside.

'You mean split up?' he asks.

'You make it sound so dramatic,' I say.

'I'm not sure our parents would like that,' he says.

'Our parents don't need to know,' I say. 'I won't say anything if you won't.'

'But we have plenty of time – we'll be able to fit in most of the biggest tourist places before we have to get back, unless you want to go somewhere that's really far out?'

I'm not big into lying. And, after today, I feel like I can trust Evan; I've seen a different side to him in Rome.

'Look, I've planned to meet someone this afternoon,' I say.

'Who?' he asks.

'A guy,' I say.

He screws up his face. 'How do you know guys in Rome? I thought you'd never been before.'

'I don't know *guys* in Rome,' I protest. 'I'm just meeting someone.'

'Is this, like, a random hook-up thing?'

'Ew, no! I've just arranged to meet someone I've met this year on holiday. It's been planned for a while.'

He goes quiet as he thinks, which of course makes me want to fill the awkwardness with more noise.

'He's in Rome today with his family, and so we planned to meet at the Trevi Fountain. That's why I didn't want to go before.'

'Is this the same guy you've been meeting up with all summer?' he asks suspiciously.

I'm smiling, because even thinking about Roscoe does this to me. 'Yeah,' I say, nodding.

But Evan looks dismayed, which seems odd.

'Anyway,' I say, when he doesn't respond to my admission. 'I'm going to head back the way we came. Shall we plan to meet up again around eight so we can get to the hotel at the same time? We'll have to arrive together or it'll look suspicious.'

'What's his name?' asks Evan.

'Excuse me?' I say. I wasn't expecting this.

'What's his name?' Evan repeats.

This will be the very first time I've told anybody about Roscoe. I didn't think in a million years that the first person I'd tell would be Evan, but I don't have anything to hide any more, so I don't see why I shouldn't.

'Roscoe,' I say, as this sweet feeling warms my insides. I brush the creases out of my T-shirt and swing my yellow bag on my back. 'So, shall we say eight then?' But he doesn't look at me, doesn't even acknowledge I've spoken. He just stares at the green water as it rolls by, as if he's seen something in there, something that nobody else can see. 'Um, hello?'

'Did you know that Emperor Hadrian lost his lover in the Nile?' he asks.

'Um . . . no?' I say, confused at the random outburst.

'According to history Hadrian cried and cried for him.' He's still staring at the green water, the light reflecting on to the corners of his eyes.

I don't know how to respond to him; he's been spilling out random Roman facts all day, but this one is jarring.

'Are you OK?' I ask. He doesn't reply. 'Evan – did you hear what I just said?'

He sits up a little taller as if I've just woken him. 'Yeah,' he says. 'I heard you. So we'll meet up by the hotel at eight?'

'Yeah,' I begin, surprised again at the change in him. 'You're sure you're OK with that?'

'I am,' he says. 'Eight. I'll see you then.'

EIGHTEEN

I use my phone to guide me back to the Trevi Fountain, but I keep an eye on the street signs too because I don't want to miss a moment of Rome. I've learnt today that the most amazing things can spring up when least expected. I'm nervous, and eager and so excited to see Roscoe. Who knew three days could feel so torturous? I don't know whether to go straight in and thank him for the postcard, or play it a little cooler and wait until he brings it up. I'm carrying my same yellow bag, so he'll know I've found it. Maybe I let him take the lead. No matter how much I want to yell my joy from the rooftops, I have to keep a level head right now.

I flip open the front pocket of my bag and take the postcard out again, stopping for a moment to admire it, his handwriting, his sweet words, and the feeling in my stomach multiplies. I think the headiness and heat, the architecture and beauty, of Rome has really got to me.

I've read that the Trevi Fountain is a wonder to behold; a modern spectacle that would put all other fountains in the world to shame. But nothing prepares me for the magnitude of it. Stone-carved columns and archways form the backdrop of a mythical scene between gods, merpeople and seahorses, growing from a rock that juts out over a lagoon, water trickling over its back. It's breathtaking and I can't think of a more perfect place to be reunited with Roscoe once again.

I make my way through the crowds until I'm at the water's edge, then I take a seat, looking over my shoulder at the illuminated pool. I notice there are coins at the bottom, and a couple standing not too far away join hands and throw one into the water. They're kissing by the time the coin breaks the surface, so they miss it. I close my eyes.

'It's beautiful, right?' I hear Roscoe whisper into my ear. 'If you throw in a coin it means you'll return to Rome.'

'Will we return together?' I ask him.

'We'll always be together,' he replies.

'Hey.'

A fire begins to rise in me as I crack open my eyes, the afternoon light bleeding through my eyelashes to reveal a face.

But the face looking back at me isn't the one I expected to see here.

'Evan?' I ask.

'We need to talk,' he says.

'Did you follow me here?' I ask, looking around the piazza.

'I need to know... What do you remember about last summer?' he asks.

'*What?* Why are you asking me that?'

This is supposed to be the most magical moment, perhaps of my life, and Roscoe could be here at any minute. I need to be happy and excited to see him, not flustered over Evan's strange questions.

'I can't believe you're doing this right now,' I whisper.

'Please, Iggy,' he says. 'Answer the question.'

'No,' I protest. 'I won't.'

'OK then,' he begins. 'I'm just going to have to tell you.' Where before he looked desperate, now he looks panicked, his words tumbling out of him so quickly they're hard to understand. 'You say you've been meeting up with a boy called Roscoe all summer?'

'Why are you doing this?' I ask, throwing my hand to my forehead.

'Roscoe,' he says again. 'Is he . . . I mean, what does he look like? Where's he from?'

'Stop it, Evan!' I shout, causing the happy couple next to me, the ones who've just guaranteed their next Roman holiday by throwing a coin in the fountain, to look my way. 'You're not going to ruin this for me.'

'I'm not trying to do that—'

'Every year it's the same – every year you do something that takes all the fun away, that makes me feel bad.'

He takes a step back, his mouth falling open. 'I'm doing this because I care,' he whispers. 'All of this has been because I care.'

I shake my head. 'Seriously? You're trying to ruin the best moment of my life because you care? Have you heard yourself? Just . . . leave me alone. You're always trying to ruin things for me, always turning up when I don't want you there. Making fun of me one moment then trying to be my friend the next—'

'I'm not!'

'You call me names, you laugh at me . . .'

He hasn't changed. He'll never change. He treats my life like it's one big joke.

He's always laughing at me.

He always laughs.

Always laughing . . .

An image cuts across the very front of my mind so quickly I feel dizzy, dulling everything else behind it; my annoyance at him, the magic of Rome and the Trevi Fountain, it all fades into the background as the harsh sound of laughter fills my head like water.

I'm on a beach, my towel spread across the warmed sand. The sun is high in a true blue sky, light dancing through the trees on the opposite bank on to my legs in flecks of lemon and gold. Someone laughs, and I see him – the Evan of last year – standing by an ice-cream shack, a gang of guys around him. He's laughing at me, calling me names, like he always does.

Then I'm running, stumbling over my legs as I approach the riverbank, danger behind me, and rushing water ahead, with no choice but to run into it. He left me no choice . . .

The laughter from the memory is his, I think.

'It was you,' I whisper. 'You're the one . . . You chased me into the river last year.'

'What are you talking about?' he says.

'I remember,' I say slowly. 'Last summer. You were laughing at me, you chased me—'

'No,' he says, shaking his head. 'That's not what happened.'

'You chased me into the water,' I say. 'It was . . . your fault. Is that why you've come here, to remind me of what you did?'

He grabs my arm and I look at his hand on my skin, at the festival bracelets and beads round his wrist. I knew there was something behind this new Evan. People don't make this much of an effort to change unless they have something to hide. Unless they're ashamed of the person they were – or *are* in his case, because he may have fooled everybody else but I know Evan Redwood better than that.

'That's not why I've come here,' he says. 'It's Roscoe – I need to tell you—'

'This makes complete sense,' I say, shutting him down. 'I knew there was a bigger reason to dislike you this year – my accident was all because of you.'

'It wasn't!'

I'm shaking; angry and scared in equal measure because I knew Evan was capable of being mean, but I never thought he could be dangerous. Never thought he would go so far. Why did he chase me?

'I could have died,' I say. 'Is that what you wanted? Is that who you are, Evan – a killer?'

'No!'

'For years you've made my life hell. But that wasn't enough for you, was it? Why stop at making someone's life hell when you can actually take that life away?'

'I'm sorry—'

'You're sorry?' I shout, ripping my arm away from him. *You're bloody sorry.* Do you honestly think that's going to cut it? Do you have any idea what you put me – what you put my family – through? This past year has been awful, for all of us, and I've spent most of it feeling guilty, or having nightmares and anxiety attacks. I've even been in therapy. And it was all because of you!'

'I'm . . . so sorry, Iggy.'

'*Oh my god!* Stop saying that. It's not going to happen – I'm never going to forgive you. Do you hear me? Never!'

I stand so we're eye to eye, so I can look at him when I say what I've always wanted to say, only I never had the courage before. 'You're a bad guy, Evan Redwood,' I say. 'You always have been, and you always will be.'

He turns and runs up the steps, out of the piazza, and I slump back down on to the side of the fountain, my heart hammering away inside me.

The woman standing next to me looks over. I'm really shaking now, hands and arms and legs. There's heat in my guts, chaos in my chest, and I need to let it out, but this piazza is full of people. I feel their gaze on me.

How could he keep something like this secret? How could he walk by my side today, how could he try to be my friend all summer, as if everything is fine, when all along he's known about this? It's sickening.

I grip the edge of the fountain, trying to ground myself, but it only makes me feel the turbulence of my anxiety even more. With so many sets of eyes on me I feel exposed. Frightened. I'm growing more aware of how monumental this piazza, this fountain, this whole city is, and I'm here alone. I'm not safe. I'm not in the camper-van with Dad and Pops. I'm nowhere near the safety of my family. I'm alone, and surrounded by strange people who don't even speak the same language.

I stand, but where am I going? I can't run. Roscoe will be here any minute.

I take out my phone and try his number. It goes straight to voicemail.

I begin to pace alongside the water as the noise of the piazza – of excited voices and rushing water and laughter, most of all laughter – grows to a deafening pitch. My ears ring, and my heart shudders, and I have to get out of here. The buildings are so tall, and there are so many people watching me, and I'm so small, and if I don't leave now I'll faint and every person here will see my true colours, will see that I'm damaged and broken, just a frightened kid.

Hurry up, Roscoe, I think.

I need him here now. I need him to wrap me in his arms and tell me that everything is going to be OK and make some silly dad joke that will make this all go away. Because I need this to go away; I need these anxious feelings to leave before they take over, because I'm scared of what's going to happen when they do.

But I can't see him anywhere. There are so many faces here, but none of them are his.

Next thing I know I'm running, fear at my back, snapping at my heels. I barge through crowds of singsong tourists, taking no care to watch where I'm going. Then I turn on to a cobbled street and run as fast as I can, as if I'm running from a monster, as if I'm running for my life. It's just like it was in the memory. I'm back there, Evan's laughter behind and nothing ahead but oblivion.

NINETEEN

I don't tell Pops, and I don't tell Dad. They look so happy and relaxed when they return to the hotel, I can't bring myself to tell them what I found out about Evan at the fountain, and how this past year of hell, of therapy and tears, was all because of him. But I can tell they know something's up; it must be written all over my face.

My panic didn't subside until I was far away from the fountain by the place where Julius Caesar was betrayed, stabbed by his friend. The irony. Although Evan was never a friend.

I messaged and called Roscoe as soon as I could think straight, but by then it was too late. As far as he knew I'd stood him up. I was the one to not show, I was the one to drop the ball. I think back to our very first meetings, by the tennis courts and then by the coach stand, and I think how crushed I would have felt if he hadn't been there. How must he be feeling right now – sad, anxious, hurt or lost? It crushes me to think of him being any of these things.

I lie awake that night, my first night in a proper bed and proper air conditioning, thinking. I think about what today should have been, how Roscoe and I should have spent the most romantic day in Rome together, and it makes me feel worse than sad. I thought summer was starting to fix me. But it turns out I'm just as susceptible to my past trauma as I ever was. It's still there, my monster, lurking in the shadows of my mind. Tonight it feels like it always will be.

I think about the memory that came to me at the fountain, and my head fills with the sound of Evan's laughter all over again. To anybody else, laughter is something fun and light-hearted. But for Evan, laughter is a weapon. Somehow this memory, and the anxious feelings it brought, makes me feel even worse than not seeing Roscoe; the pain is deeper, coming from a fragile and broken place inside me. If Evan hadn't followed me to the fountain, none of this would have happened.

Today would have been the perfect day it was always supposed to be.

But then, the truth had to come out sooner or later.

The question I keep coming back to is why. There must be a reason why he chased me into that river. What did I do to Evan Redwood that was so bad? Was this a homophobic attack; does me living as my most authentic self offend him so much? But then chasing me into a situation that so nearly cost me my life feels extreme. Maybe he is just a bad guy. And bad guys do bad things.

The one thing I'm sure of is I'll never forgive him. Even if I can get over what he did last summer, which at this moment seems unlikely, I'll never forgive him for what he did this summer, today. I'll never forgive him for taking my last day with Roscoe away from me.

The next day when we're sitting across from each other on the train back to the campsite, I keep a dignified silence for my parents' sake. When he looks at me, his eyes big and searching, I look elsewhere. When he offers me a seat, or stands so I can get past him, I don't acknowledge him. It's as if he isn't here.

Make no mistake; this is far from over. I'll deal with him when I'm good and ready. But Evan Redwood ruined the last summer for my family. I'm not going to let him ruin this one too.

TWENTY

After Rome we begin the slow journey home. Summer is very nearly over. Our next stop is Milan, which is inland. Then we will head through Switzerland to France. The next time we see big water it will be the English Channel. I'm already pining for the magic of the Med. I'm not ready for home; the thought that we're travelling north, when I know Roscoe is heading home, crushes me.

We never got to have our last evening together in Rome. We never got to make plans about what happens when we get back to the UK. I try his phone again, but it goes straight to voicemail, and all my messages go unread. As it stands, it could be weeks – maybe even longer – until I see him again, and with no way to get in touch with him, it's left me feeling lost. I've never known a summer to end so abruptly. It's as if the last few weeks never happened, because I'm back to feeling like the old Iggy; the Iggy from home, the frayed-around-the-edges version of the person I used to be, the person I *have* been this summer. I thought I had moved on a stage in my healing journey, but this blow has knocked me way back. I'm wandering through the dark, in need of his jokes, his kisses, his touch more than ever, but I don't know when, or even if, I will see him again.

It's left me thinking that maybe I wasn't healing at all.

Maybe it was all just him.

We reach the campsite early evening. We don't set up as we usually would; there are no fairy lights, or gazebo. We'll only be here for two nights before we head further north to Switzerland, so there's no point in settling. The settling part of our holiday is long over; we're now in our nomadic phase, following Pops' itinerary all the way home.

'You're not yourself today,' he says as I emerge from the camper-van. 'Are you feeling unwell?'

'I'm fine,' I mumble.

'I'm going to get pizzas for tea,' he begins. 'What would you like?'

'I don't mind.' I smile at him, and it takes more effort than a smile should.

He has his map of Europe spread out on the table. He runs his finger diagonally through France, and I'm reminded of that day in the kitchen before we came on holiday, of how nervous and excited and hopeful I was. I can't believe we're heading home, and this is how summer is going to end. It feels so unfair.

'Come and sit by me,' he says, pulling the nearest chair out.

I do as he asks and take a seat on hard plastic.

'I'm looking at our route to Paris,' he says.

'I still want to go to Dijon,' I say.

I've come this far; I'm not going to back out now. I still want to return to the place it happened. I still want to gather up whatever scraps of memories are left there, if only to find out why Evan Redwood did what he did. There is a part of me that thinks I'm only torturing myself by going, but just because something is hard doesn't mean it's to be avoided. It's not like I can see Roscoe now, so all I have is this.

'We can't get a pitch on the campsite,' he goes on. 'But we have the option to stay at a farmhouse down the road. It won't be exactly like it was last year.'

'I don't need it to be exactly like it was,' I say. 'I just need to be there.'

'OK,' says Pops, nodding slowly. 'I'll make arrangements to stay in the farmhouse.'

I push the chair away with the backs of my legs and stand. As I do, a thought comes to me; it may not be only me who's apprehensive about returning to Dijon: Pops might not be asking only for me, but for him and Dad too. Last summer was horrible for all of us, maybe even more so for them because they lived through the trauma every day. I was pretty out of it for a long time, but they were wide awake through it all.

'I'm sorry,' I say. 'I know this is probably hard for you and Dad.'

He shrugs. 'This isn't about us,' he says.

'But it is,' I say. 'You guys remember more of it than I do. It must have been really tough for you, and I'm sorry if any of those feelings come back.'

'Don't worry about that,' he says, gripping my hand. 'If you think going back there will help you in any way, then your dad and I are here for you.'

Tears prick the corners of his eyes and he looks back down at the map.

I instinctively bend down and wrap my arms around him, because he may be my Pops, he may be the parent, but everybody needs a hug when they're upset. I feel so bad that he's crying, and this is when I'd feel the usual stab of guilt. But as I grip on to Pops as tightly as I can, I realise that his tears are because of one person.

I don't think I've hated Evan Redwood more than I do right now.

'I'm fine,' says Pops, wiping his cheeks, sitting a little taller. 'We'll go to Dijon and have a wonderful, healing time, and then celebrate the end of the holiday in Paris.'

'I've never been to Paris,' I say.

'I know,' he says. 'You'll love it, Iggy. It's the most fabulous city in the world, the City of Love.'

I kiss his cheek and then shuffle around my chair.

'I hope you find what you're looking for, Iggy,' says Pops as I walk away. 'You deserve to be happy.'

'Me too,' I say, and I feel something tug me on the inside as I think about Paris being the City of Love, and not being there with Roscoe. And I don't see how I can be happy.

Not now.

TWENTY-ONE

I've thought about Dijon a lot this year, probably even more than I've realised. I've been anticipating my return ever since I knew we would be coming back to France, and so, as the green road signs start pointing towards Dijon, I begin to feel strange. I don't know what I expected to feel. I knew excitement would be inappropriate, but I thought there would be some sense of relief. I thought my mindset would be entirely positive, if not a little apprehensive. But as the numbers of kilometres on the road signs get smaller, I feel my unease turn up a notch.

The farmhouse we're staying in is twenty minutes outside of the city. As we turn on to the dirt track that leads to the little courtyard out the front, I notice the Redwoods' camper-van already parked up.

'You didn't say the Redwoods would be here,' I say, leaning forward towards Pops.

It's going to be hard enough being here without having to deal with Evan. Sitting across from him on the train is one thing, but sleeping under the same roof is another.

'Of course they're here,' says Pops. 'They've had the farmhouse booked for months. How else do you think we managed to find rooms so last minute in August? Look, Iggy, it's still summer. We're still all going to Paris together.'

It's still summer, I think. *But it doesn't feel like it.*

We roll to a stop and I see Julie, Dave and Evan standing in the courtyard, waiting to welcome us.

'You made it!' sings Julie as Dad winds his window down.

'That was a long one,' he says. 'What time did you get here?'

'Around thirty minutes ago,' says Dave. 'Did you see the storm clouds over Beaupont?'

As Dad and Dave talk about their journey here from Geneva, I glimpse over at Evan. He looks dreadful, like he hasn't slept or eaten in days. His eyes are bloodshot and ringed, and his summer tan has turned a shade of sallow. He looks gaunt and small, and I'm guessing this is down to guilt. I don't want to feel bad for him, and I shouldn't feel bad for him, but there's such a faraway look in his eye that I can't help it.

'How are you, Iggy?' asks Julie as I step out of the van, folding my arms across my chest. It's definitely a few degrees cooler here.

'I'm good,' I say.

She grips the top part of my arms and presses her lips together, which I take to mean 'you're brave for coming back here'.

'It's a lovely house,' says Pops.

'Gorgeous, isn't it?' says Julie. 'We haven't chosen rooms as we weren't sure who wanted to be where.'

'I'm not sharing,' I say, not even trying to be discreet about my rude outburst. I need it known from the get-go that there's no way I can be shacked up with Evan here, simply no way.

'Iggy,' says Pops.

'Nobody needs to share,' says Julie. 'There's enough space for everyone.'

I carry my bag in through the open door and step into the house. The rich smell of woodsmoke comes to greet me as I walk in. This is thanks to a big fireplace, the insides charred black and dusted with ash. Two sofas face each other in front of it, and in between them sits a coffee table with board games stuffed on the shelf underneath. Behind the sofas there's a long dining table, made from dark wood, and behind that a dresser full of dishes.

'How charming,' says Pops, walking in behind me.

In the corner of the room, a spiral staircase climbs up to higher floors.

'Is that the way to the bedrooms?' I ask.

'Yes,' says Julie. 'There are four upstairs and one down here just off the living room.' She points to a door in the back wall.

'I'll take the smallest one,' I say. 'Unless anybody has any objections?'

I look at Evan when I say this, who is standing sheepishly by the doorway.

He shakes his head.

'That's upstairs at the end of the landing,' says Julie.

'Thanks,' I say, and then I make my way across the room and climb the stairs to the next floor.

At the top of the stairs there's a corridor with a wooden dresser and a jug of sunflowers on top. I walk over the creaking floorboards that dip in the middle from old age, to the door at the end. Inside the room there are two single beds, a bedside table's distance from each other, and a square window that opens out on to the courtyard. I dump my bag on the bed under the window and take a seat.

And it's as if the whole world stops. I'm here; I've arrived in the place I've thought about coming for so long, and now I don't know what happens next. The world outside the window is the quietest I've ever heard, with no roads or people nearby. All I can do is sit here in the silence and wait for something to happen. If something happens.

I reach my hand into the front pocket of my bag and take out Roscoe's postcard.

Iggy, I hear him whisper as I hold it to my chest.

I lie back, my head finding the pouffy feather pillow, and gaze out of the window on to the courtyard and the fields beyond it. I'm feeling so much, and I don't know where to start in processing it all. I miss Roscoe. I wish there was a way I could speak to him, but he still hasn't read my last message. I doubt his phone is even switched on. There are so many questions hanging over us; about what we are, and whether we'll see each other again, and the uncertainty has me on edge. I'm also back here, in the place where my accident happened, waiting for some sort of recognition to come flying at me, wondering if it actually will, or if coming back was just a huge mistake.

And on top of it all, I'm sleeping under the same roof as the person who ruined the last year of my life, the person who took a practical joke too far, or thought chasing me into a river would be funny, or whatever was going through his head at the time, and nearly cost me my life.

Lying here all night is preferable to sitting downstairs at the dinner table in this charming French farmhouse and making conversation with someone I can't even look at right now.

So I stay put.

I don't go down for dinner. I don't get freshened up, or change out of my travelling clothes, or make any kind of effort at all. I just lie here, until the sky turns dark and the stars come out and sleep eventually finds me.

I wake in the night to a strange sound. It starts quietly, like breathing, maybe in the next room. I sit forward, my head cocked to one side as I try to hear through the wall. The sound grows. It isn't coming through the walls. It's here. It's in my bedroom. It's inside my head. I throw off the bedsheet, peeling away the soft cotton so the chilly night can find the bare skin on my legs. Then, standing in the middle of the room, I listen to it. It's moving, growing; it seems further away now, like it's coming from outside. I lean across the bed to poke my head out of the window. The night is alive with cricket song, with moonlight and whispering breezes.

One of the whispers says: *Iggy*.

It shudders across the field just beyond the fence, running with its arm outstretched behind as if it would have me take it, as if it wants me to follow. But where, I don't know. Do I dare do as it asks, even though I know I'm not supposed to? I wait in the dark, held still by invisible hands pressing on my shoulders.

This is why I came here, I think. *This voice has the answers I've been looking for. All I have to do is follow it, as easy as placing one foot in front of the other, and it will do the rest.*

I creep down the spiral staircase, the sound of my parents' snores, the most comforting sound, pressing against my back as I descend. Pops would call me back right now; he'd tell me to go back upstairs to bed. But I haven't come all this way to stay inside, behind closed curtains, under the covers. I've come for answers.

The living room still smells of supper, of tomatoes and red wine and garlic. I creep past the dining table, remnants of red speckled across the tablecloth, place mats still out, empty bottles grouped together in the middle. It looks like everyone had a fun dinner. How did I sleep through it?

The key is in the door; I turn it once and then yank the heavy wood towards me.

The noise is louder out here; it's higher pitched, mixed in with the strings of cricket song. A full moon hangs, fat and round and red, above the farmer's fields. It looks like a ripe peach that I could pick from the sky as easily as from a tree. This makes me think back to the orchard in Provence where the peaches were small and unripe. Now they're ready to be picked; now they're ready because now I'm ready.

Beyond the boundary fence lies a forest. As I approach the trees, the sound intensifies; it sways the branches, bends them, as it rustles through leaves.

Iggy, it says. *I'm waiting here for you.*

I grip the wooden fence and swing my leg over the top, and then I jump down on to the other side.

It's darker here in the forest where the light from the stars and moon can't reach. I'm left to feel my way through, to grip rough bark and trip and stumble over exposed roots. But still I keep going, keep pushing forwards all the way to an opening where a river cuts through.

Here, lit by moonlight, standing at the water's edge, is where I find him.

'Roscoe?' I say.

His face lifts into a smile as soon as he sees me. 'Iggy,' he says. 'I knew you'd come.'

'What are you doing here?' I ask.

He reaches out a hand. 'Come here. Let me show you.'

It's as if our hearts are magnets. We're drawn to one another. We're yin and yang; he has the thing that will complete me, and I need it. I need him. I couldn't stop now even if I wanted to. I take his hand. It's colder than stone. He doesn't feel like him, he doesn't look very much like him either; his hair is loose about his shoulders and his cheeks are pale and drawn.

'Are you ready?' he asks.

'Ready for what?' I say.

'Ready for what you came here for,' he says, looking down at the rushing water that sweeps up everything in its path. 'The truth.'

LAST SUMMER

TWENTY-TWO

There's something about morning sunlight on holiday. It means something different. At home, sunlight means getting out of bed for school. Sunlight means no more time spent sleeping, wrapped in my blankets, a head still buzzing with dreams. Sunlight means the end of something. But when the sun shines through the camper-van window, on to my bed, it feels different. It's the same sun, but this morning, as a cockerel crows from the farmyard next door to the campsite, and the sun, already hot, shines on to my face, I can't wait to throw away my bedsheet and head out into the world.

I think Roscoe Jones might have something to do with this.

'You're up early,' says Pops as I step out of the camper-van, into the morning.

He's sitting at the table, sipping a cup of coffee. There's a plate of fresh croissants in the middle, their pastry all shiny and golden. I reach forward and grab one, and then I take a bite. Like the sun, I think croissants are better in France.

'What are your plans today?' Pops asks me.

This is another thing that's different about holidays. Freedom. Back home, I'd be restricted by curfews, or family plans, or piano lessons, but here I'm able to plan my day. I'm able to choose how I spend my time.

'I'm going to the reservoir,' I say.

'Again?' he asks, because I've gone to the reservoir every day this week.

'You get a better spot if you go earlier,' I say.

'Who are you going with?'

'Just some friends,' I say.

'Evan?' he asks.

I roll my eyes. 'What do you think?'

'Will you be there all day?' he asks. 'Do you have enough euros?'

'Yeah – probably all day. And yeah – I'm sure I'll be fine.'

I grab another croissant because they're so good and one just isn't enough, then I head along the path to the campsite's main house.

'Keep your phone on!' Pops shouts after me.

I raise it in the air because it's already in my hand.

Roscoe is waiting at the gate for me.

'Bonjour!' he says, holding out his arms.

It sounds funny in his Welsh accent, so I have to laugh.

'Bonjour,' I say back.

When I get close enough, he hugs me. It feels nice to be hugged by him, feels nice to be so close to him. I've never liked anybody like this before. I've had crushes, of course I have, but admiring from afar, sitting on the outside looking in, is a world away from the real thing. And Roscoe feels like the real thing; he's warm hands, and deep-voiced, and his touch ripples through me like water. I never thought a summer romance would be on the cards for me. But something magical has happened to me this summer for the very first time.

At one end of the beach there are rows upon rows of neat sunbeds and umbrellas, while at the other it's a bit of a free-for-all, where the sand meets the water on one side and a cliff face with a forest on the other. At this end of the beach you don't have to pay for sunbeds, all you need is a towel. And they have the best ice-cream huts.

My flip-flops sink into the sand as we walk across it, towards our own quiet corner, where we lay out our beach towels side by side. I like this place because it feels secluded, our own private beach where we can be ourselves away from the crowds. Roscoe and I both love the water. We actually met for the first time in the sea. His paddleboard collided with mine and we connected right away. In a romantic way, I like to think the water brought us together, like in some ancient story in Roman or Greek mythology. It's like the world wanted us to meet, like we were supposed to.

I've never wanted someone so much. It's wild. How is it possible to feel this way about somebody I've known for a little over three weeks? This is the most excited, the most magical, I have ever felt in my life. I can't think about summer ending. I can't think about the day I have to return home, the morning sun waking me up on a normal school day, trying to shoehorn myself back into that life when I've grown and evolved into this person who is filled with so much life.

'What are we going to do?' I ask, my hand lightly brushing his arm.

'Do?' he asks.

'When we leave here, when we get back to the UK. I . . . don't think I can be without you.'

He smiles. 'What are you talking about? You'll never be without me.'

He grips my hand and I fold into his side. I know this doesn't answer the question; this doesn't deal with the practicalities of how I'm going to get through Year Eleven without seeing him every day, but his words still help to ease the sting of sadness in my stomach. No, it isn't that. It's rounder than that, made in a deeper place. Heaviness. That's what it is; a heaviness that presses on my insides, because our time here is nearing its end. This is a downside to travelling to so many different places over the course of the summer; the number of times I have to say goodbye.

The reality is we can't see each other every day. We can't even see each other every weekend. I want it to be just like it is now. I want summer to last forever. I want to live in a world of summer nights, kisses and warm touches. I want France to be my forever, because what's waiting for me back in the UK doesn't look anywhere near as appealing.

'When I get back, I don't start school for two weeks,' I say. 'That's plenty of time to come to Wales.' He removes his sunglasses and turns on to his front, rolls into the shade so he can look at me properly, but he doesn't say anything. 'I'm being serious,' I continue. 'I need to see you.'

'You would come to Wales? To see me?' he asks.

'Of course I would.'

He begins to think about something, thoughts as big as the Mediterranean Sea moving behind his eyes as he disappears inside his head. I want to follow him in there. Wherever he goes, I want to go too. I'd follow him anywhere.

'What is it?' I ask.

'It's just my parents,' he says. 'I know they wouldn't approve.'

'I don't think I can be without you,' I whisper.

He reaches forward and grips both of my hands. 'I can't be without you either,' he says. 'We'll never be apart for long, Iggy.' He strokes my cheek, and I lean my head into his hand, where the bracelet from Marseille is tied to his wrist.

'I promise you,' he says, cupping my face.

Before I know it his lips are on top of mine, and we're kissing. His warm hands move over my skin, and I melt like ice cream left out in the sun.

'*Get a room,*' someone shouts.

I open my eyes to see Evan Redwood and his gang of 'guys', pointing in our direction, laughing.

'Are you two a couple then?' shouts one of them.

'Just ignore him,' says Roscoe.

'I'm pretty sure that's impossible,' I say.

Evan smiles at me, and I know that smile. It isn't a happy or warm smile. It's a smile that says *I'm about to screw you up.* I've seen that smile way too many times. He walks across the sand towards me, his guys following close behind him.

'Is this who you've been disappearing off with all summer then?' he asks.

'Number one,' I begin, 'I haven't been disappearing anywhere. And number two – I didn't know you cared.'

A flush of colour runs across his cheeks and the guys laugh.

'I don't care about you,' he says. 'Don't flatter yourself.'

'Don't spy on me then,' I say. 'Don't you have anything better to do?'

'Yeah, I do,' he says.

I hold my hands out as if to say *then go and do it* because this is our special place, our private corner of the beach and I won't let Evan taint it for us.

'Fine,' he says.

He turns back towards the ice-cream hut, but one of the guys keeps staring, an angry look in his eye. He looks at Roscoe, then he looks at me, then mutters something in French under his breath.

'Who was *that* guy?' asks Roscoe.

'I don't know,' I say, shaking my head. 'I've never seen him before.'

'Did you hear what he called us?'

'No. Did you?'

He shakes his head, although I don't wholeheartedly believe him. The guy obviously said something mean, only Roscoe doesn't want me to know what.

I lean forward and kiss him again. 'Where were we?' I ask.

'We were planning our future,' he says, winking at me.

'Oh, that,' I say, sighing. 'We get back to the UK on the twenty-fourth.'

'Then I'll see you on the twenty-fifth,' he says.

'How?' I ask, half laughing.

'I don't know,' he says. 'I'll find a way. I'll walk to Northumberland if I have to.'

'It'll take you a while . . .'

'My point is, there are ways around this, Iggy. Tell me now – do you want to be together?'

'Of course!'

'Then that's what's going to happen; I'm putting it out into the universe. *Do you hear me, Dijon?*' he says with his full chest, his voice carrying across the reservoir. '*Iggy and Roscoe aren't going down without a fight!*'

'Shhh!' I say, jokingly placing my hand over his mouth.

'Do you believe me, though?' he asks. 'Do you believe that no matter what, I'll find a way to be by your side?'

'If I say yes will you stop shouting?' I ask.

'Maybe.'

'Then, yes,' I say. 'I believe you.'

I'm prepared to fight for him, for us. That I even have to do that scares me, I can't deny it, and the summer days seem to be rushing away from me, slipping through my fingers like sand, but I believe the love between us is strong enough to sustain us. It has to be.

TWENTY-THREE

That night I sit at the dinner table, thinking about Roscoe. Now that we've talked about what comes next, set the ball rolling towards our future, I'm feeling all kinds of content. I'm meeting him at the beach later, which has become our thing here in Dijon, and so for now I'm floating, lifted above the table by the feather-light wings in my belly. Tonight, a few of the usual families have joined to have a barbecue. We've each placed a picnic table into the middle of the walkway that separates our different pitches, so it looks like we're getting ready for a banquet. Pops has made a table display for the middle from some of the wild flowers that grow in the neighbouring fields. He's twisted them around the citronella candles we use every night to keep mosquitos at bay. He's tied some coloured ribbon around our glass jugs and filled them with juice, and placed napkins on each plate.

We have three different barbecues on the go, and the smell of smoke and charred meat thickens the already thick evening air. It's nice, and I like it when we all come together like this, but at the same time I kind of want this meal to be over so I can see Roscoe. This is what I'm like now; a couple of hours away from him and I get fidgety as he begins to infiltrate my every thought.

I wonder where he is now.

I wonder what he's having for tea.

I wonder if he's thinking of me.

When the first round of burgers and sausages are ready, piled high on two plates at either end of the table, I grab a bun and dig in. There must be about twenty of us eating tonight, which isn't unusual. As I bite into the meat and bread, I think about what it would be like to go on a family holiday with just my parents, like Roscoe. I would miss this, the feeling of community when we eat at the end of the day. Maybe I could convince Roscoe to come with us next year; maybe we'll celebrate a year of knowing each other back here in France next summer. That would be awesome, actually: coming back here to France, to the place where we found each other for another month of sunshine. I wonder who we'll be this time next year, wonder if Year Eleven will change things.

I'm just about to enjoy my second helping of burger when Evan Redwood joins the table, taking a seat opposite. He throws me this irksome smile; short, sharp and pointed, but I don't throw it back. I have far more important things to think about right now.

'Good evening, Evan,' says Pops. 'How was the reservoir?'

'It was good,' he says, through a mouthful of burger.

I grimace at him. I can't stand people talking when they're eating.

'I actually saw Iggy,' he says.

'Oh?' says Pops. 'Did you two hang out today?'

'Yeah, it was so great to see you, Evan,' I lie. 'What was the name of your friend again? He's so fun.'

'I'm far more interested in *your* friend, Iggy,' he says, fluttering his eyelashes at me.

I should have expected this from him. Why didn't I think about it before now? Of course Evan was going to use what he saw on the beach against me. Of course he was. When has he ever been able to resist telling my parents my business? The guy is a perpetual nuisance, designed to irritate. Before now I was able to swat him away like a fly. Before now, the stuff he'd told my parents about me – like when he told them I cried during the tennis tournament because I was no good at it, or when he told them I find it hard to make friends – weren't anywhere near as important as this. He can't tell them about this. He can't. He'll ruin everything; our plans, our future, everything.

'Oh, who's your new friend, Iggs?' Pops asks.

'Just someone,' I shrug. I'm not talking about Roscoe and me yet. We're keeping us under wraps out of respect for his parents. If they find out then it could be the end for us. Seriously. So, yeah, Evan needs to stop talking.

'I think he was more than a friend,' says Evan.

I stop chewing; stop breathing, I think. I didn't think it was possible to dislike him any more than I already do. But this takes things to a whole other level. This is my life. And I won't stand for anybody coming between Roscoe and me, and certainly not Evan Redwood.

I'm going to have to fight dirty too.

'I'm surprised you noticed,' I begin. 'You were too busy being cautioned by the police, weren't you?'

This makes the entire table fall silent, which means I kinda have to commit myself to this lie now.

His mouth falls open. 'What?'

'What was it you stole again?' I ask.

'I didn't steal—'

'I mean, I think it was only a few bits and pieces from one of the shops, but still – shoplifting is a serious offence. Especially in France,' I add, dramatically. I don't know if this is the case, but it sounds good.

Evan's dad marches over to his chair.

'What's this, Evan?' he says.

Evan shakes his head. 'I didn't.'

'Although, saying that,' I continue, 'it must have been more than a few bits if the police were called. I'm not surprised he didn't tell you . . .'

Dave Redwood's face turns a darker shade of red, as Evan looks from him to me. 'You're lying!' he says. 'I didn't steal anything! You're just trying to divert like crazy because I saw you kissing that guy on the beach!'

I swear my heart stops beating.

All at once my ability to lie, to play dirty like him, leaves me. All at once I'm fumbling, and useless, with shaking hands and a racing heart. Every set of eyes around the table falls on me, including my parents, and I don't know what to do. Should I deny it?

'Shut up, Evan,' I say through gritted teeth, slamming my hands on the table.

'No – you shut up!' he shouts. 'And stop telling lies!'

I stand. He stands too. And there's no way I'm going to back down to him, not now.

'What are you so embarrassed about?' shouts Evan. 'Just tell everybody about your new boyfriend.'

'Piss off, Evan!'

Pops appears at my side, gripping my arm. 'That's enough,' he says.

But it's too late.

I've already stuck my hand into the bowl of potato salad, I've already gripped a fistful of it, and I've already launched it at Evan's head.

The next thing I know, Evan is standing across the table from me, potato salad dripping down his face on to his T-shirt.

Everything goes quiet, even though I know Pops is shouting at me. I know Evan and his dad are shouting at me too. But I can't hear them. They're screaming underwater, the noise unable to reach me. I'm immune. I'm numb. I'm gripped by something I've never been gripped by before. Is this what rage feels like? I've never known anything like it. It's as if some dial has been turned up inside me and it's blocking out all the noise.

In my dream-like state I begin to walk away, turning my back on raised voices and chaos, even though I've caused it. I've lit the touchpaper, but I'm not hanging around for the explosion. I leave everything behind and make the leap between here and there, with no idea where I'm going to land.

That's if I land at all.

I know the way like the back of my own hand. *Left out of the main entrance.* As I walk, my calm rage turns into frantic anger – I'm so mad at Evan for ruining everything. *Along the road.* Why did he have to do that? Why does he always have to be such a terror? *Turn right at the sign.* I'm never coming on one of these holidays again, not if he's here. No way. *Head downhill all the way to the reservoir.*

It looks different in the evening, with sunbeds stacked and secured behind the ice-cream hut and the sand raked evenly so there are no footprints. I look out over the water as it ripples through blue, orange and red, reflecting the rapidly changing sky, and I feel a piece of my anger dislodge, leaving more room for other feelings to take precedence. I'm colder now, apprehension placing a hand on my shoulder because I'm wondering what's going to happen. Can I go back there? Pops and Dad will be so mad.

I walk across the sand to the water's edge, allowing the water to wash over my sandals. This feels like a disaster of epic proportions. I feel like something in me has been wrenched apart. My heart? I don't know. How could Evan do this to me? If this means the end of Roscoe and me, then I'll never forgive him for as long as I live.

Roscoe, I think.

I want him here now. I need to tell him everything that happened at dinner. I need him to talk me off whatever ledge I'm on, because I can only see this as a disaster. I would give anything to have a boat right now. I would give anything to be able to sail away with him, leave everything behind and escape. He's all I want. I'm so mad that Evan has threatened what we have. I'm so mad that . . .

'Hey.'

But it isn't Roscoe I see when I look back. He isn't the person who's come to the beach to rescue me.

It's Evan Redwood.

'*You?*' I say. 'What are you doing here? Get away from me. I don't want to talk to you.'

He's changed his T-shirt already.

'I want to talk to *you*,' he says.

'I have nothing left to say to you,' I say, turning away. Facing the water will keep me calm, and I need to stay calm right now. Roscoe will be here soon. 'Do you have any idea what you've done?'

'I'm sorry,' he says.

'You don't even know what you're apologising for,' I say. 'You have literally no idea how serious this is.'

'I do. I know how serious this is – it wasn't my place to tell your parents about you.'

'No – it wasn't.'

'I'm really, *really* sorry. I didn't mean to. You just make me so mad all the time . . .'

'I make *you* mad?' I say over my shoulder. 'Are you joking right now?'

He appears at my side and I take a step further away from him, releasing my feet from the sand.

'I . . . want to tell you something,' he says. 'I . . . No, I need to . . . Well, I want you to know that . . .'

'I don't want to hear it,' I say, turning to face him. 'Seriously, Evan – you've already said way too much tonight.'

But he doesn't move. He stays at my side, looking at me as if I'm an animal in a zoo or something; as if I'm some wild thing. Part of me wants to lash out. Part of me wants to show him just how wild I can be. The potato salad might just be the start. Who knows what else I'm capable of when I feel this mad.

'Just leave me alone,' I whisper.

Again, he doesn't move, so I take this as my cue to walk away from him, to move further along to the other end of the beach. I need to stay calm and think of a way out of this, but my mind won't stay still for long enough for me to do so. I need Roscoe here.

Walking across the sand seems to take more effort than it does during the day. During the day this beach is a fun place for sunbathing, and ice cream, and pedalos. This evening, every footstep in the dry sand seems to push me another one back, as if I'm moving in a dream; running somewhere but getting nowhere at all. The sand is heavy and hard to manoeuvre, settling between my toes, coarsely rubbing the skin away from them.

I make it to the dirt path, and I'm just about to turn on to the road when I hear voices, raised voices. I shuffle to the edge of the path so I can hide behind a tree. It's then that I see them, a group of guys probably around the same age as me. They're yelling at each other, or someone, but I can't quite make out what they're saying.

Until . . .

'Where's your boyfriend then?' asks one of them.

I swear my heart turns solid; turns into something that isn't meant to float inside a person's chest, surrounded by other squishy things, but a rock, too heavy to carry, because I can make out Roscoe's colourful shorts and his favourite D&D T-shirt. It's him these guys are shouting at, ganging up on him.

'Just leave him,' says another, and I recognise Evan Redwood immediately. He must have taken a shortcut through the dunes.

This makes me step out on to the road, the anger I feel towards him still with me, still enough to give me the courage needed to keep moving forwards, to push me towards them.

'Is there a problem?' I shout.

The group turns towards me.

'Here he comes,' says someone. I recognise this guy; he's the guy from the beach, the one who muttered something to Evan today. He has a mean face; he's all dark-ringed eyes and shadows. 'Come to meet your boyfriend, have you? Are you gonna kiss him again?'

I don't stop walking; I don't allow him to scare me. I walk up to Roscoe and grip his arm firmly, standing at his side.

'I don't see how that's any of your business,' I say.

'You were happy to kiss him on the beach before,' says the guy. 'Go on, do it again.'

I pull Roscoe towards me so we're even closer. 'Come on,' I say. 'Let's get out of here.'

We go to walk off but the guy comes between us, shouldering Roscoe in the chest so he stumbles backwards.

'What do you think you're doing?' I say, turning on him.

But before the words have even left me, Roscoe is on the ground, the sound of dry gravel crunching and scraping as the guy restrains him. He swings his hand up, clenching it into a fist, and then he lands his first punch right on the side of Roscoe's head.

What happens next is so quick I feel like I'm watching it play out in a film, looking at my life through a screen. The other guys jump on Roscoe, but then I dive in and pull two of them off. The other guy still has him on the ground. He reaches into his shorts and pulls something out. A knife. It glimmers red as he holds it up to the light of the setting sun. I scream. I'm scared. I'm really, *truly* scared. I lunge at him and grab his hand, sinking my teeth into him so hard I draw blood, the taste of iron dancing across my tongue. He releases his grip on the knife and I kick it across the road. Then someone else jumps in and wrestles him off Roscoe. It's Evan.

'Run!' he shouts at me. 'Both of you – run!'

I lunge forward and grab Roscoe's T-shirt, pulling him off the ground. There's a cut on the side of his head, blood running down his face on to his chest. The two other guys go to grab him too, but with strength I didn't even know I had I shoulder both of them out of the way, sending them flying into the ditch on the side of the road.

Then we run.

I hold Roscoe round the waist and we hurry as quickly as we can away from the attack, downhill, past the beach and the reservoir. But they're not going to stop. I hear them running behind us, hear their heavy breaths and shouts as all three of them herd us away from the sand and towards a forest.

'I don't know where to go,' I panic. 'Roscoe, where do we go?'

'That way,' he says. 'We need to keep going that way.'

He takes my hand in his and then pulls me forward, running through the trees, long branches whipping at my skin. We run, and trip and jump over uneven ground, cutting a path through as best we can, but all the while we can hear them behind us, closing in on us.

The trees open out and we find ourselves on a riverbank. Below us, the brown water moves rapidly as it twists through this dark forest.

'There they are!' someone shouts behind us.

'We have to cross,' says Roscoe.

'We can't,' I say, looking down at the water. 'It's moving too quickly.' I know water. A river moving as quickly as this will swallow us up as soon as our feet leave the riverbed. 'There has to be another way.' I look up and downstream. The river is wide and we have no idea how deep it is.

The trees behind us begin to snap and move, as the gang swipe their way closer to us, laughter piercing through the dark.

'Come on!' says Roscoe.

Then we begin to manoeuvre our way around slippery rocks, keeping tight hold of each other's hands as we edge ourselves carefully into the river.

'Don't let go of my hand, OK?'

We wade in further until the water comes up to my waist, and already I can feel its power; already I know that the undercurrents are strong. 'We can't swim,' I say. 'We have to float. If we can just find some driftwood, or—'

'There isn't time,' he says.

I edge closer to him, and something clips me and I lose my footing. Suddenly I'm moving away from him, the water running away with me downstream as I grip his hand as if it's all there is in the world.

'We should turn back,' I say.

'We're nearly there,' he says, pulling me into him. 'Stay close.'

We edge towards the other bank, where trees hang low towards the water. *If I could only grip on to a branch then I could pull us across*, I think. But they're still so far away. The water is at my chest now, and I'm finding it harder to keep upright; we're in far too deep.

All at once Roscoe's head goes under, and I feel his grip tighten in my hand as the water pulls him away from me.

'Roscoe!' I shout.

My heart begins to pound in my chest as I stare at the constantly moving water, my insides constantly moving too. He breaks the surface, and I can see that he's disorientated. He didn't expect the river to be so strong; he doesn't know water like I do.

'Roscoe!' I shout, pulling him closer. But I'm fighting against the current, and it's too powerful.

'Don't let go!' he screams.

But his grip is loosening. I can see our hands beneath the surface, stretched out ahead of me, and they're sliding apart.

'Roscoe!' I shout again.

'Help!' he cries. 'It's pulling me in! Help me! Please!'

Something tugs him sideways, and our grip weakens. I'm up to my chin now, the water bubbling towards my mouth.

'We need to turn back!' I scream.

It's the last sound I make, because suddenly my head goes under.

I struggle under the surface, trying to move towards what little light is left. But the water is so dark. I'm confused and scared. I swim as hard as I can until my head pokes through the surface. My eyes burn as I look around for anything

I recognise: the forest, the riverbank, Roscoe, but I don't know where I am. Fighting against the river is impossible. I kick my arms and legs, trying to keep my head above the surface, but a current comes from behind again and pulls me under, turning me upside down and sideways and around, water flushing into my ears so I can't hear. I kick as hard as I can but I don't find the surface again. I'm swimming into colder waters, going down instead of up. But I can't stop. I need to breathe. I need air. My chest is starting to tighten, my ribcage going into spasm as my lungs try to expand on their own.

And this is it.

This is all I am.

I'm panicked and powerless. The water can do what it wants with me. It flushes into my body with great speed. In an instant I become something else, part of something bigger, controlled by some force that's beyond my comprehension. I become the water. I become tidal. I become something other than I am. I'm no longer Iggy Caddock, no longer anything. The light is fading because I'm fading, easily now, like falling asleep.

Thoughts come with so much space between them I lose the concept of time. There could be a week, or a month, or a year from one thought to the next, I couldn't say.

And then it comes; my last thought before the light goes out, my last ever thought. It's one of calm. I think about Pops and Dad. I think about how much I love them, how much I'll miss them, how I wish I'd told them every day just how much. Crazy how that happens when it's far too late. I think about how surprising this all is, how I thought it would be more painful, more violent. But it's easy. This is really easy. Effortless.

It's amazing how inevitable this feels; it's like, why was I taking life so seriously when it was always going to end? What was I fighting for? Why did I go to all of those piano lessons and after-school activities? Why did I try so hard when I was always going to lose?

It seems so stupid now, when there's nothing left.

Only darkness.

TRUTH

TWENTY-FOUR

For a suspended moment I'm nothing. There are no more feelings. They've all gone; I've been wiped clean of them.

Blank. Numb. My hands don't look like mine. My arms don't look like my arms; there are more freckles and moles and hairs. I'm changed. I'm older. A year has gone by, and I can't remember a moment of it. Not really.

The first thing that comes back to me is awareness. It rattles around inside my head, like the first penny in a jar. I become aware of my extremities, my fingers, elbows and toes. The penny rattles and parts of me start to awaken, as if I'm waking after being asleep for a long time. The next thing I notice is my heartbeat; the second penny. I begin to feel its power as it flushes life through me, fluid pushing and pulling this way and that, as if my blood is the river. Then feelings wash over me quicker than I can recognise them: touch, taste, cold, fear, and ones I don't even have names for. The sand feels hard and coarse in between my fingers as I grip the ground. It hurts me, makes me sad. I realise I'm on my knees, my head bent over, staring, just staring. Somewhere nearby there's a noise; a bell ringing, I feel it clanging in the very top part of my stomach as it violently swings one way and then another. I begin to sway with it, as if I am that bell, being thrown from side to side with no rest in between. The feeling in my stomach grows heavier, and I'm too many things at once; waking up far too quickly now, and I can't handle the speed at which I'm becoming me again, fast as hummingbird wings, as my heart gathers speed.

Then I throw up.

With streaming eyes and scratching throat I throw up again and again, the muscles in my back aching as I lurch forwards on to the sand as my body empties itself.

Then I'm on my side, the hard grittiness of sand in between my teeth, looking at the world, a vertical line between the sky and the earth; stars and moon on one side, riverbank, mountains and trees on the other. There is no sound, only my breath, howling in my nostrils like the wind.

I don't know how much time passes; could be a minute, could be an entire year, there's no way to measure time here in this strange sideways place where the horizon slices the world right down the middle. The trees sway up and the river flows backwards here. Time is measured in heartbeats and breaths here. I am measured in other things in this new world I don't recognise; I'm weight and texture; earth, water and air. I float in the calmness of it all, feeling everything and nothing all at once. Feelings are listless creatures here, their claws dragging behind them with nothing to cling to, no memories to ground them, to grip and feed upon.

Beyond my feet, the river is rushing by, moving with speed as it smooths the stones on the bank. This is when it comes to me: memory; the final part of the jigsaw, the final penny in the jar. This is when I remember everything. This is when

I become Iggy again, and my feelings have something to sink their teeth into.

I feel each bite.

'*Roscoe*,' I hear myself whisper.

I keep staring at the water, at how quickly it's moving, at how strong the current is. You'd have to be very smart, or very lucky, to survive it.

But surviving doesn't feel lucky; I survived, didn't I? That's what happened. I survived that night, and he didn't. They found a boy in the river the next morning and it was him. It had to be him. That means I'm the lucky one. Right? Only, how can I be lucky when Roscoe is dead?

I lurch forward as if I'm about to throw up again, but nothing comes up because there's nothing left. I'm dry-retching, my feelings snagging on my throat, but not able to get past it.

Roscoe is dead, I think.

I feel my insides shift, a canyon opening up somewhere, as my heart breaks cleanly, perfectly in two.

There never was a guy on the paddleboard the first night of the holiday. There never was a guy to dance with me in the town square, or stargaze in the peach orchard. He wasn't there in the medieval tower, or cliff diving in Saint-Tropez, or in the boat in Baia di Paraggi. There were no sunlit kisses, or late-night meetings or talks of the future, not this year

because I lost him last summer,

and I didn't even know it.

'*Iggy – what are you doing?*'

Someone grabs me from behind, falling to the sand so they can hold me. I don't struggle against them; I don't push them away so I can be alone with this. I collapse into them as I cry hard and loud. The tears come from the earth, come from deep roots, rushing through my body and out of my eyes. I cry and scream as I feel this loss in every part of me; my back, my legs, my teeth ache under the pressure of feelings that are big as the sky.

'Iggy, what were you thinking?' someone asks.

I shake my head, and then the only words that come are, 'He's gone.'

How could I forget him?

This memory is overwhelming enough, but the *realisation* that comes with it; knowing that I forgot about him for a whole year, brings something else, something darker, something that I don't know if I'll be able to forgive myself for.

'Your parents didn't know about him, did they?'

I shake my head. 'Nobody knew,' I say. 'He was the first guy I'd loved, and nobody knew about him.'

'I did.'

For a moment the noise of remembering stops, and I'm left feeling curious. *I did*. This person knew about Roscoe, knew about us. How?

I pull away from them and chance a look at their face.

'Evan?' I whisper.

The moon shines a spotlight on him, on his sad eyes and facial hair. He doesn't look how he did in the memory of last summer. He doesn't look that way at all now.

'I didn't tell them,' he says. 'I wouldn't do that ... I tried to make it right. Those guys ... I didn't want to hang out with them, but there was nobody else and you didn't want to ... I tried to make them ease off, but this one guy just wouldn't, and so that night, when we saw Roscoe heading to meet you, I knew something would happen. I didn't realise he had a knife. That's why I alerted your parents. That's why I told them to call the police. I was . . . so scared.'

He's talking to me in a dream. That's how it feels, anyway. I'm in this strange, suspended place in between the memory of last summer and now. I watch his face; watch tears fill his eyes, watch spittle gather in the corners of his lips as his words become so thick he struggles to breathe life into them. He looks different to the guy I knew. No, it's more than that. It isn't just about the way he looks. The way he's talking, the way his emotions are flowing out of him, the way he's still holding on to me so tightly, makes him seem like a caring person. Is it possible I've got it wrong about him too?

'You alerted my parents?' I ask.

'Right away,' he says. 'I knew those guys were going to take it too far. I didn't realise how far. I never would have left you if I'd known what was about to happen . . . and then all of a sudden you were gone, and the emergency services were called, and they searched the riverbank for hours until they found you.

'Your parents asked me what happened, and I told them you wanted to swim. I'm sorry. I wish I'd been brave enough to tell the truth. Wish I'd been brave enough to say that the guys I'd been hanging around with all summer made this happen. But I wasn't. You were taken to hospital. I didn't know what happened until days later, when we were in the port in Calais. I was watching TV, and this French news reporter was talking about how a body had been found in some case for a lost schoolboy. They called him Jack. Jack *Roscoe* Jones, and the picture on the screen was him. I . . . didn't know what to do. I wondered if I should say something. But if I told my parents what I knew, it meant telling them about your relationship, and I wasn't sure if that was OK.'

I begin to draw lines in the sand with my index finger, lines that begin to resemble a word. Or, rather, a name.

Roscoe.

He seemed so real.

I don't mean real as in vivid – like when you wake from a dream and you know it was a dream but you can still see it clearly, maybe even feel some of the stuff you felt while you were dreaming it. This is different. He was here. He was with me. I felt his touch, his warmth, smelt his skin, held his hand, kissed his lips. He helped me, rescued me, did things there's no way I could have done on my own. He was very, *very* real.

'I saw him,' I say.

Evan doesn't respond, but I can feel his dubiety.

'I don't mean for a brief second but then it actually turned out to be someone else,' I say. 'I *saw* him. I've been seeing him for weeks. I . . . thought we'd just met this year, thought he was real.'

'I know,' he says.

'Am I . . . crazy?' I ask.

'You've been through a lot,' he says.

'But to see him so completely . . .' I say.

I instinctively grip the earth again, burrowing my fingers into it, grounding myself. I've dreamt about the day my memories of last summer would come back to me. I imagined the dark cloud that's been with me since, then lifting, and the sun coming out, and joy returning and summers going back to how they used to be. This isn't like that. It's more complex, more conflicting.

'What happened after?' I ask Evan. 'When they found Roscoe – what happened after?'

'I'm not sure,' he says. 'We didn't hear anything about it on the news back home, or anything. It was bigger news over here – French story for French news channels, I guess.'

'But weren't there questions asked about how it happened?' I ask.

'I don't know, Iggy,' he says.

'Didn't anybody wonder how he ended up in the water? Didn't anybody connect him being found to me being found in the same river?'

A look of confusion crosses his face. 'They . . . questioned you, Iggy,' he says. 'Don't you remember?'

Returning to the broken memories of last summer lands differently now. Now my head is above the surface, bridging the gap between taking my last steps into the river with Roscoe, and taking my first steps out of bed in a French hospital ward, it feels easier. Pictures begin flickering in my mind. *First image.* There's a guy in a shirt and tie. He was a translator, I think. Next to him is a woman wearing a suit. She asks me questions. The guy translates. And I answer as best I can. Pops stands behind. He looks worried. No, this is something else – he looks *surprised*, like he doesn't understand why they're questioning me about the death of some poor schoolboy. *Second image.* The guy is talking to me again. His shirt is a different colour. It's a different day.

He holds up a picture. I recognise Roscoe's face. But I don't feel anything. The memory doesn't come with feelings. There are only these flickering images. There one minute, gone the next. I don't think that I – the person in the hospital bed – recognise the face looking back from the iPad the guy is holding. He swipes the picture to other images; a Dungeons & Dragons T-shirt, a bandana, and a black leather bracelet with *Marseille* stitched into it. Pops looks from the iPad to me, waiting for me to acknowledge any of these images, but I feel myself shaking my head, because I didn't recognise these things then. I do now. *Third image*. The guy shakes his head at the woman. They both look disappointed. They say goodbye to Pops and Dad. They aren't coming back.

'I couldn't tell them anything,' I say. 'By the time I woke up, I couldn't remember him.' I stand too quickly, a shadow blurring my vision as my blood rushes to my head. 'I should tell them,' I say. 'The man and woman – the translator and the detective – they need to know what I know. It's not too late.'

I head for the forest that leads back through the field towards the farmhouse. I want to run but I can barely walk.

'Where are you going?' asks Evan.

'To tell somebody,' I say. 'He can't just be . . . forgotten. I need to tell them.'

I have to tell somebody, anybody, about him, about us. This, right here, was the reason I wanted to come back to Dijon. These memories have to mean something, have to *do* something. Don't they? He can't be some stupid kid who went in the river at night and then died in a tragic accident; he was so much more than that. He was so much more than that to *me*. He showed me things, and made me feel feelings I didn't even know existed. He was universal energy that came into my life, and everybody needs to know just how seismic he was. Everybody has to know what happened, and how brave and caring he was. He was too special to be forgotten. I . . . I loved him. In whatever short amount of time we had, I loved him. I still love him.

'Wait. Iggy – stop.' Evan grabs my arm and pulls me back. 'What are you going to do – post on Instagram about a guy who passed away a year ago?'

'Of course not,' I say. He makes it sounds so callous.

'Then what? Are you going to seek out his family? Put them through even more heartache?'

I hadn't thought about his family. I never met them, just like he never met mine. We weren't together like that. In our world, there was only us; we were each other's sun and moon. Our world had only two people in it. Now there's only one, there's only me.

'I should go to Saint-Tropez,' I say.

'What?' he asks.

'I should speak to her,' I say. 'Grandma Edith – I should tell her . . .'

I trail off as I think about that day. Grandma Edith saw him; she held his hand and whispered to him. How was that possible? Was I hallucinating or did she see him too? *Really* see him? Maybe the veil between what's real and what isn't was thinner for Grandma Edith; maybe that's what happens when a person comes to the end of their life. Maybe he was as real to a dying woman as he was to me.

'It's over, Iggy,' Evan says.

'But I have to do *something*!' I say.

'Calm down,' he says, his hands taking hold of my shoulders. I'm shaking, cold fear shivering in my joints.

'Come, sit down,' says Evan.

'No, Evan!' I snap. 'You have no idea what this is like. You have no idea what it's like to be so—'

'Scared?' he says, cutting me off.

There are tears in his eyes, and I don't understand them. Why is he crying? This isn't about him. He didn't know Roscoe. He barely knows me, not really.

'I've been scared every day since it happened,' he says. 'I've had to live with myself, knowing that I played some part in this, knowing that maybe I could have done more. I'm probably the only person who does know how important last summer was. So let me help you. Please.'

A tear rolls down his cheek at the exact same time one rolls down mine, and it's like we're feeling the same thing, mirroring each other's emotions like we're mirroring each other's tears. It's like I'm looking in a mirror right now and Evan is another version of me, maybe even a future version of me, who's a year down the line, living a year away from this night, a year away from remembering everything.

'How can you help me?' I ask.

'Someone died, Iggy,' he begins. 'And as far as I was concerned, you had some sort of brain damage, and it was my fault. So, yeah – I do know what it's like to feel so scared, and to see no clear way out from those feelings. So let me be the person that I needed this year for you.'

I failed to see that when I stepped into the river last year the ripples stretched so far, and it isn't only me who's been living with the cloud of last summer hanging over them; Evan Redwood has too.

I nod, slowly at first and then more assertively. He was the last person I would have thought about talking to. But now I know the truth, now I know what he did, I think we can both be what the other needs. It's like we're both carrying a broken piece of the same thing, and we need each other to put those pieces back together again, to fix it, only neither of us knew what the other had until now.

He puts his arm around my shoulders and moves me away from the riverbank. Turning my back on this river feels significant. I don't need this place any more. I'm done. I've cast my net into the water and reeled in the thing I've wanted to catch for months: the truth. But what happens now? Do I just sit back and wait for my joy to fall into my lap? That's what Sian Steadman's quote in the golden frame alluded to. Finding joy should be easy as finding the truth.

But then, this truth, my truth, is a whole lot more complex than that.

This truth doesn't come with a joyful release; it doesn't bring with it sunshine through rainclouds, but only a greater storm.

TWENTY-FIVE

As I lie listening to a dawn chorus of birds, cows and a crowing rooster, as the sky turns from night to day, I feel the grief sitting on my chest, and I wonder how I'll ever stand up from this bed when it seems so heavy. I go back to the beginning, to the day I first saw Roscoe when our paddleboards collided, and I wonder how a person who wasn't really there can seem so real. My thoughts turn like a wheel of fortune, sometimes taking me high as I think of peach orchards and Saint-Tropez, but then always dropping me back down again. I don't have answers, and I don't know if I ever will, but of one thing I'm certain: he's gone. Whatever bridge he made, between last summer and this one, or between my waking and dreaming state, or between the living and the dead, I know for sure that I won't see him again. With the truth I so desperately wanted has come a change I so desperately wasn't ready for, and now I'm stuck wondering how I'm going to do this.

Feeling it a year later doesn't make it any easier. I still want to see him. I'm still thinking about a life together back in the UK. I'm still thinking about birthdays and Christmas and even next summer, and what's even more screwed up is that I don't know how to stop myself. So I just lie here, going round and round. I should have done more. If only I'd pulled him back, if only I'd kept hold of his hand. If only we'd chosen a different path and ran alongside the reservoir instead of heading into the forest. So many thoughtless decisions amalgamated into something catastrophic, and it didn't have to be that way. He didn't have to die.

I think this is what stings the most; that he could be here right now, maybe even on holiday with my family. The year I've been planning for us could have been the one I've just lived through.

'Iggy?' says Evan, his eyes cracking open on the next bed. He didn't think I should be alone. 'Are you OK?'

I don't answer him; just keep staring at the ceiling, willing myself to be stronger and not fall down the rabbit hole of my imagination. I've imagined an entire summer, it would seem. I need to stop somewhere. I need to stop now.

'It's morning,' he says, looking out of the window. 'Did you manage to get any sleep?'

I shake my head. 'I don't know how I'm going to do this,' I hear myself say. My voice sounds scratchy and dry.

'Do what?' he asks.

'Any of it,' I say. 'It feels like too much.'

'Give yourself time,' he says.

'How much time?' I ask. 'A month, a year, a . . . lifetime? When will I forget about this?'

The irony isn't lost on me that now I've remembered, I want to forget again.

He sits forward and swings his legs over the side of the bed. Then he begins to scratch at his beard, the sound of fingernails brushing against coarse hairs breaking up the noise coming from outside the window. 'For me,' he begins, 'it didn't become about forgetting about it completely. It became about learning to live with it.' I tilt my head towards him so my head is sideways on the pillow. 'I found that it didn't just go away – rather, I built an imaginary wall around it.'

'A wall?' I ask.

'Yeah,' he says. 'So whenever what happened that night came into my head – and it still comes into my head every day – I had something in place to stop me from getting upset.'

'I don't understand,' I say. He's talking about building walls when I've spent the last year trying to knock them down.

'If I feel myself slipping into it,' he continues, 'I begin rationalising, and then talking positively to myself – *you tried your best, you're a good person, you did the right thing* – sort of thing, and over time these things became more important. It's been kind of like working a muscle, counterbalancing the dark thoughts with positive affirmations.'

I feel bad that things got so dark for him that he had to do this. I also feel bad that I've been so stand-offish with him this year, when he's been struggling too.

'Why didn't you tell me?' I ask, because, as far as I'm aware he's had nearly thirty days' worth of opportunities to tell me. At any point he could have put me out of my misery and stopped me from sinking further. But he didn't.

'I wasn't sure what you remembered,' he begins. 'And my parents told me to go easy on you this year. As far as they knew, you were suffering from PTSD. Every time we spoke, I looked for a way in, but then it became clear you'd forgotten so much, so I left it. Then I saw you on your own outside the campsite next to Portofino, and it looked as if you were talking to somebody, and I wondered if you'd really left all of last summer behind. It wasn't until Rome,' he continues, 'until you told me the name of the guy you've been meeting up with, that alarm bells started ringing.'

'The *imaginary* guy I'd started meeting up with,' I say. What have other people been seeing when I thought I was with Roscoe? I must have looked so pathetic talking to myself all summer. 'Get it right.'

He shakes his head. 'Don't be hard on yourself about that,' he says. 'Whatever you saw, whatever you imagined, it's nothing to be embarrassed about. It makes sense that your brain would connect this summer with the last one.'

'But it isn't normal,' I say. 'It isn't normal to spend all summer with the memory of someone. How am I supposed to trust myself now? How do I know what's real and what isn't? Am I even talking to you right now, or did you die last summer too?'

I'm scared that I can't trust my mind. Will it happen again? Am I living in a perpetual horror film where I see dead people, going about their business, walking around like regular people, unable to tell the difference?

'I think part of me did die,' he says. 'But it was the part that needed to die – it was the stupid kid, who thought it was funny to call people names.'

'Yeah, well, that's one person I *am* glad to see the back of,' I mutter.

I rub my hands down my face and sit forward, the blood rushing to my head. I feel empty, and light, as if my insides have been scraped out and all that's left is a shell. I don't know how I'm going to get to the end of summer in one piece, never mind what comes after, when I feel this fragile.

'You won't always feel this way,' says Evan, as if reading my mind. 'I promise you – a day will come, somewhere in the future, where this won't feel so big. I believe in you.'

I reach forward and take a sip of water from the glass on the bedside table. The water moves through my empty insides, like a river, making pathways in places that feel dry and desolate. I'd like to believe him. I'd like to believe that everything will work out in the end, and that there's no reason to feel scared because the way I feel now won't be forever. But, truthfully, I don't know if I can.

Young people aren't supposed to die. That isn't how it works. Life isn't supposed to end so suddenly; there's an order to things. Death is supposed to be a gradual trail of hospital visits, and treatments, and good news, and bad news, and looking on the bright side, and then accepting there's nothing that can be done. It isn't supposed to be like this. Someone who was so new in my life shouldn't leave so soon. Roscoe should have been around for a long time, maybe even forever. I can't get my head around it. I feel like Alice trapped in Wonderland; everything is the wrong way up, and nothing looks as it did even yesterday, and I don't know where to begin in setting everything back to how it was.

Maybe this is the point.

Maybe things aren't supposed to go back to the way they were, and this is the very first day of my new life.

Gaudium in veritate, I think.

But how can I possibly find joy in any of this?

Evan stands from the side of the bed and yawns deeply as he stretches. 'I can smell bacon,' he says, sniffing at the air. 'Someone must be cooking breakfast.'

I can hear Pops and Julie downstairs, their voices accompanied by the sound of clattering pans.

'Should we go down?' he asks.

'I'm going to stay here,' I say. 'I don't feel much like being with people right now.'

He walks over to the door. 'Do you want me to bring you anything up?' he asks.

'No,' I say. 'Thank you.'

He opens the door, a stronger smell of breakfast wafting into the bedroom, and then heads along the corridor, the floorboards creaking with each one of his steps.

As soon as I'm sure he's gone, I fall backwards on to the bed.

Which is where I stay for the rest of the day.

TWENTY-SIX

Our time in Dijon bulldozes on, one long day in the farmhouse bleeding into another. While Pops suggests going into the city, or to the reservoir, or heading out for a walk through the surrounding countryside, I stay in bed, drowning in my emotions. I feel bad, because I wanted this; I pushed for Dijon. But I didn't give a thought to what would happen when I remembered. I wish I could snap out of it, for them more than anything, but my feelings are too dense. I was supposed to find a way out of them this holiday, and Dijon was supposed to provide the antidote to this past year, but my life is just as small here as it is back home. It's frustrating, and annoying, and upsetting, but I don't know how to get beyond it. My therapy toolbox is empty; I've thrown everything I can at this, and still I feel so bleak.

And all I keep thinking is that he, Roscoe, would know how to pull me out of this. He's the only antidote I need. He could make me laugh right away, or cup my face or kiss me and everything would be right again. But he's gone, and every time I think about him I feel his loss all the more.

So here I stay, in the farmhouse, in the small bedroom at the end of the corridor while my family, and the Redwoods, try to carry on with their summer as best they can.

Pops doesn't leave me. It's just like it was in the hospital. Dad takes care of me too, bringing food up to my room and sitting on my bed, but Dad is better when he's doing things. Pops is more vigilant, quietly there in the background. Every morning I see him from my window, sitting at the table in the courtyard, reading articles on his iPad, or sunbathing. He looks sort of sad on his own, which makes me feel worse. I don't want his summer to end like this. I don't want this to be how this year ends. I wish with everything I have that I could make these feelings disappear, but wishes feel useless against feelings this big.

What makes it even harder is that I know Roscoe wouldn't want this for me. Roscoe wasn't about darkness. He wasn't about closed curtains and lost days. Roscoe brought the sunshine with him; he made everything feel like a new adventure, and when I was with him I always felt so good. Laughter buzzed around our heads, like an irritable bluebottle. Now he's gone, now his light has gone out, it feels like mine has too.

I wish there was a way to switch it back on.

But God. It hurts like hell.

We should be planning our next adventure. We should be thinking about colleges, and maybe even beyond that. He had his whole life ahead of him; he could have gone on to do great things, had a family, and lived a full and colourful life. Our entire future has been ripped away, with no care or gentle word to soothe the pain.

When I think of him I hear his voice, as if he were sitting at the end of my bed, whispering to me as I sleep. I drift away on a paddleboard, my mind transported to the south of France, and then I wake, suddenly, covered in sweat, my cheeks wet with tears, looking around the room for him.

Then I remember.

And the cycle of grief begins again.

And still I can't believe he's gone.

TWENTY-SEVEN

The next day I go for a walk.

Both of my parents, and even Evan, offer to come with me, but I want to head out on my own. I don't want to fill the afternoon with words; with conversations or questions about how badly I'm feeling. I want to get away from that. I want to lose myself in the French countryside, in something much bigger than the inside of my head, and see what I find in the silence.

I follow the dirt track, which has yellowed in the sun, away from the farm buildings until the countryside opens up around me and there are no more buildings, or cars, or houses, or people, only miles of open fields, bordered by wild flowers and grasses and trees. As I walk, the sound of my trainers crunching against gravel, I think about Roscoe, and after a mile or so of sadness, my thoughts begin to surprise me. I feel the glow of last summer here, out in the world. As I brush my hands through green, red, purple and yellow flowers, and walk past sunflower fields, and horses lazing in their paddocks, I think of the day I met him. In my mind's eye I see bright water and pebbled beaches, the sound of jet skis and speedboats buzzing across the horizon behind us. I think about how surprised I was that he wanted to talk to me that day, and how he flirted with me right from the beginning, and I smile. I see our secret meetings; by day in the gift shop in Marseille, when he took out a Sharpie and wrote our names on the shelf with the rest so we could be there for always, and by night when the stars came out, and he could name every one. I see us out on the reservoir in Dijon, not too far from here, in a pedalo, the day I fell overboard and we laughed so hard. I can still feel that laughter, the best laughter I've ever known, bouncing around my insides. I find myself smiling so broadly, and laughing through my nose. I can't help it. That's what he did to me whenever I was with him.

This is how I want it to be, I think. I want to remember the laughter, the smiles, the good times; I don't want to remember only sadness. He was so much bigger than sadness. Last summer ended tragically, but that doesn't mean it was tragic. Last summer was filled with joy, and I don't want that to disappear because of how it ended. I know I've been living inside my head, inside these memories, but in a way I'm glad that I got to experience him all over again. I got to feel him again; feel his warmth, his touch, his kindness in a way that all felt so real. I want to keep the memory of last summer alive. I want to keep the memory of *him* alive. Thanks to him, I know the sound of my own laughter. I know who I am when I fall in love. I know how I feel when I'm watching the sunset or naming the stars. He revealed parts of me I'd never met before. If he were here right now he'd probably grip my shoulders and make me stare summer dead in the eye. He'd tell me to enjoy every moment instead of drawing the curtains because the sunshine feels too bright.

For a brief moment I swear I can smell him, smell sun-blushed skin, and doughnut sugar, as if he's standing next to me, holding my hand as I take my first step on a path I've never walked down before.

God, I miss him.

When I get back to the farmhouse, I find Pops and Dad sitting at the table out the front.

'I'm back,' I say, walking up the path towards them.

'Hello, darling,' says Dad, looking up. 'How was your walk?'

'It was nice,' I say. 'It was great, actually.'

I hesitate for a moment, as I summon the courage to speak. I've decided that now is the time to tell them everything. It takes me a minute to get my thoughts in order, because I've become so used to hiding them. Now I'm not hiding any more. Now I want them to know everything about the guy who came into my life and made so many important changes. I want them to know what the last year of my life has really been about.

'Can I talk to you both?' I ask.

'Of course you can, my love,' says Pops.

I scrape out a chair. 'I have a few things I'd like you both to know,' I say. 'And you're probably going to freak out, but I want you to know that I'm fine. Or at least, I think I will be.'

'That sounds worrying,' says Dad.

'What did I just say?'

'Sorry,' he says, removing his sunglasses.

'We're all ears,' says Pops.

I sit a little further forward in my chair. 'I want to talk to you about last summer, about what happened and about what I remember . . .'

Words flow out of me. I go back as far as I can, remembering details about things I haven't had access to for such a long time. I talk about Roscoe, how we met, then the amazing times we shared together in the south of France, and here in Dijon. I talk about what happened the night we ended up in the river, not too far from here, and how I survived that night but he didn't. I tell them what I remember about being in hospital, and how I knew they were both at my bedside even when I was asleep, things I've never opened up to anybody about.

Then I tell the story of this summer, and how I met Roscoe again, how I fell in love with him again, and how somehow he helped me find my lost joy again. I tell them about Roscoe, but I also tell them about Evan. Evan, who I thought was the bad guy but was there for me in a way no one else could be, who's surprised me the most this summer.

'I don't want either of you to feel sad,' I say, reaching out to grab both of their hands, because Pops looks like he's about to cry, and Dad's eyes are so open and sad. 'That's not what this is about, and that's definitely not why I'm telling you. I know it's a tragedy that he died, but I want this to be about joy. It has to be about that, otherwise it's just more of the same; this tragedy will go on forever, and before I know it I will have spent my whole life in therapy, feeling scared and uncertain, and I don't want that to be my life. I've seen enough of the dark this year to last me a lifetime. I want to be happy now. Now I know – now you both know – everything that happened, I want to move forward on to better times.'

'Oh, Iggy,' says Pops.

A red admiral butterfly appears out of nowhere and lands on our hands, and I catch my breath. It opens its wings wide so I can see the red, black and white print, which looks so bright in the sunlight. I don't think I've ever seen one this close before, never seen the details; how their backs look silver, or how their wings are trimmed with white frills. I look from it to Pops, who's staring with wide eyes, a distant, childlike look across his face.

'Did you know they sometimes only live for a day?' I say. 'They pack everything into such a short life, bringing so much joy to so many, and then it's done.' I look at Pops. 'Do you remember what you used to say about butterflies?'

'Yes,' he says, his voice cracking.

The butterfly's wings flutter, and then it gently lifts off my hand and disappears into the sky. I close my eyes, a breeze rushing past my ear, stroking a warm hand against my cheek as it whispers my name in a voice I will never, *ever* forget.

'Death ends a life,' says Pops, 'but it can't end a relationship. Not if we choose to keep it alive.'

This makes me smile. That's Pops all over, always searching for the rainbow.

JOY

TWENTY-EIGHT

Evan and I catch an early train in from the campsite. We're only here for today, and then it's Calais in the morning for home. Although, something tells me that the home I'm returning to might feel a little different to the one I left behind.

The streets are busy as we step out of the station, the sound of cars and motorbikes whizzing past. This city has a character of its own: classy and sophisticated, but with a rebellious heart that yearns for romance. Where Rome was earthy and ancient, Paris is refined, fine-pointed and demure. It's hot. Of course it is; it's Paris in August, but there's also a gentle breeze swaying the tops of the trees that perfectly line the riverbank, which reminds me that summer is nearing its end. There's a weird synchronicity about this happening on a riverbank. It gives today more power, and makes the closure all the more clear for me. As soon as I see the Seine, the ancient river, twisting through the city, I know that this place will forever hold meaning for me.

We walk along the banks, where artists paint and the giant towers of Notre-Dame cathedral stand guard, and I look in the distance to see the Eiffel Tower, its bronzed pinnacle stabbing into a watercolour sky; a landmark structure for a landmark day in my life, I think. The Pont des Arts bridge sparkles in the distance as the sun shines on the many padlocks that have been fixed there. They glisten like fish scales, each tiny link making up something greater than itself, making something beautiful. There are so many more than I thought there would be. The pictures did this place no justice. It's overwhelming, but in a nice way, because each one of these locks represents love. They are a physical embodiment of something; a moment locked in time. This is where I'm going to leave my very own moment. This is where I'm going to leave a constant reminder of us.

With the end of the holiday only days away, I knew I was running out of time to honour him, to honour us, in a way that held meaning. I wanted to buy a keepsake to remember him by from a gift shop in Dijon, the place where he passed. Then I thought about visiting a gift shop in Paris. But nothing felt quite right, until I remembered the gift shop in Marseille, the one where people from all over the world left their mark on the shelves, and how instead of taking something to remind me of him, I could leave something behind. Something here in France so that a part of us stays here for always too.

I take the lock out and hold it in the palm of my hand. It was at a market in Troyes, the last place we stopped before Paris, where I found an engraver to write our names on it. Iggy and Roscoe. I know that the path ahead is going to be tough, but if I ever feel overwhelmed I can always take a trip to Paris.

'There,' I say, noticing a gap in the middle of the bridge, the perfect spot. I like the idea of the lock being in between two sides, like his world and mine, which somehow crossed over this summer.

I press the padlock against my lips. I close my eyes and feel the cold metal against my skin. I can smell him, smell his windswept hair and sun-warmed skin. I ache for him. I didn't even know this was a thing, didn't even know that you could miss someone so much. But I can feel him in my bones; the joints in my fingers, my spine, my jaw, as if he's here right now, at my side, his hand holding mine as I make this grand gesture for us.

'I'll never forget you,' I whisper, my eyes closed.

Maybe I had to forget him to remember him again. Maybe letting him go had to happen this way. I don't know if I can believe that his presence really was with me this summer, and I don't know if it matters all that much anyway. All I know is that I was sleepwalking for a long time, and now I'm awake again, and it's thanks to someone who changed me in such a way, I can never go back to the person I was before.

I fix the lock to the bridge with one sturdy click, then I pull the key out of the bottom and throw it into the river.

'It's done,' I say, watching the water.

'I'm proud of you,' says Evan, placing his hand on my back.

His face breaks out into a smile that says so much. The corners of his mouth and eyes lift and I see gratitude and relief. I'm not the only one who needed closure, I think.

'We can move on now,' I say. 'Both of us.'

I take Evan's hand in mine and we walk away from the bridge. It feels nice to walk away from this river. It eases the sting of remembering; it eases the sting that losing Roscoe all over again has brought and makes me think that there is a pathway out of this for me.

A pathway blazed by Evan Redwood.

I think about how lonely this past year has been. I think about how much I needed someone, only I didn't know. I think about how that person was Evan all along. I never thought the day would come where I'd be happy to feel so connected to him. But as the Parisian sunshine shines on our backs, all I can think is how I'm so glad he's here.

'We're going to keep in touch, aren't we?' he asks. 'I know we never have before, but I feel like things are different now.'

'Yeah,' I say, nodding. 'I would like that.'

It feels like a fitting ending to this summer, one that somehow also feels like a beginning. In a strange way, I've felt like my life has been on pause. I spent a long time waiting; waiting to remember, waiting to feel normal again, and then I spent a long time fearful of what the waiting meant. I felt trapped, and often hopeless, controlled by a past I knew nothing about. Today marks the first step towards my future. I know I have my issues, but I also know where they come from now.

I know the shape of this monster. I know it isn't lurking mysteriously somewhere in France; it's out in the open, the mystery is over, and so it can't scare me any more. I know my feelings aren't dangerous or anything to fear; they're rooted in something tragic and traumatic, and I own that. I'm going to walk away from this city today, and every day that comes after it, owning that. That doesn't mean it's going to be easy; it doesn't mean I'll never think about what happened again. But it does mean I'm not afraid anymore.

And when the dark days show up, which I'm sure they will, I'll think of summer, and then I'll come back to the only thing that really matters.

Joy.

ACKNOWLEDGEMENTS

First and foremost, I'd like to thank my parents. Mam – your constant belief in me is, quite frankly, astounding. I can't tell you how grateful I am for you. Dad – you're always on my side, and you give the best advice. I come away from spending time with you, usually on one of our long walks through the Northumbrian countryside, feeling like I can achieve anything. I'd like to thank my grandparents – Andrew and Despina Tawse, and Robert (Bobby) and Jean Glen – whom I felt keenly while writing this book. Thank you for telling me stories. I'd especially like to thank the Greenwood family – Chris, Beverley, Alex, Victoria and Katherine – for the most incredible summer memories. I'd like to thank Tom, for being so utterly dependable, and my wonderful friends – Tricia, Roxanne (Sheila), Lizzie, Steven, Stella, Michael, Charlie, Anna and Kieran. I couldn't do this without you!

To Becky Bagnell at Lindsay Literary Agency – thank you for your belief in me and for introducing me to the team at Hachette UK. For this I'll be eternally grateful. To Georgina Mitchell, my editor at Hachette Children's Group – your energy and ideas have contributed so much to this story. You've blown my mind with this book! To Lena McCauley – thank you for giving me the opportunity to share my stories. To desk editor Laura Pritchard and copyeditor Hazel Cotton – thank you for polishing this story until it shone. To Joana Reis – thanks for the brilliant cover design and for being so open to my suggestions. I'd also like to thank Dominic Kingston, the teams behind BKMRK and Hope Publicity, and everyone at Hachette Children's Group who's had a hand in making my dreams come true.

This story is inspired by family holidays I went on as a teenager, caravanning in France and Spain. It was on one of these holidays that I bought my very first diary, a silver pocketbook from a gift shop in northern Spain, which changed my life forever. I think it's interesting that I started writing during my teen years, when it so often felt like I had to hide my true voice. Writing saved me then, and has done every day ever since. I'm grateful for the holidays and adventures, and most of all I'm grateful for the little silver pocket book, which began the greatest adventure of all.

Photo © Ben Wulf Photography

Daniel Tawse is from Newcastle. They spent their childhood going on adventures in the wilds of Northumberland, and teenage years writing diaries about how much they didn't fit in. Nowadays, Daniel spends their time turning those diaries into stories for a wider audience, and is an advocate for queer representation and visibility in the arts. Through their work, Daniel aims to provide authentic queer characters to demonstrate positive and relatable queer voices for all readers. Elsewhere, Daniel has studied theatre at the Arts Educational Schools, London, and holds a master's degree in British History from the University of Northumbria.

❎ 📷 @DanielTawse

ALSO BY DANIEL TAWSE

Roman Bright has always loved love stories. But so far, the search to find a love interest for their very own sweeping romance has been totally hopeless. Being an openly queer, non-binary teenager in a small town means their dating pool is limited.

So when postcards and colourful graffiti signed by someone called 'Big Red' start showing up for them at school, Roman is shocked to discover they might have a secret admirer ... Roman *thinks* they know who is leaving these messages, but will they finally get their happily ever after?

DON'T MISS

Rocket Middleton is broken-hearted. The love of his life has unceremoniously dumped him, just when they were supposed to be starting a new life together in London. Crushed, Rocket heads to drama school alone, where Emmy Star, the biggest young musician of the moment, is training for an upcoming film.

When Rocket first meets Emmy, sparks fly, but could a famous young musician *really* be interested in Rocket? Then, just when Rocket thinks he might be starting to move on, his ex shows up again. They don't call it *drama* school for nothing ...

Want to be the first to hear about the best new teen and YA reads?

Want exclusive content, offers and giveaways?

Want to chat about books with people who love them as much as you do?

Look no further...

Sign up to our newsletter now!

See you there!

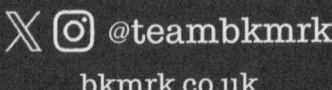

bkmrk.co.uk